PRAISE FOR *Gem & Dixie*

A *Publishers Weekly* Best Book

A Brightly Best Book

"With a vivid, well-rounded cast of characters,
including the adults, and a poignant portrayal of family dynamics,
Zarr's frank, resonant story is both bittersweet and triumphant."
—ALA *Booklist* (starred review)

"Gem's prickly, agonizingly real internal monologues
quickly bring readers into her corner, and her messy, layered
interactions with Dixie are heart-wrenching.
As the unpredictable turns of events progress, Gem's quietly
growing convictions about her own future are hard-won and
nuanced. A poignant and smart family drama."
—*Kirkus Reviews* (starred review)

"Zarr movingly explores the effects of neglect
on two vulnerable girls relearning how to trust.
Readers' hearts will ache for Gem, who so desperately wants
to follow a different path than her parents, as she tries to
carve out a better life for herself and her sister."
—*Publishers Weekly* (starred review)

"*Gem & Dixie* is a beautiful, poignant, and ultimately hopeful story
from one of the finest YA authors writing today.
An exploration of the complicated love and loyalty between sisters
that is at once profoundly moving and unflinchingly real."
Nova Ren Suma, *New York Times* bestselling author of
The Walls Around Us

"Zarr adeptly brings to life a protagonist grappling with anger,
loneliness, and rejection. The siblings' relationship is authentically
nuanced. A thoughtful work that will resonate with Zarr's many fans
and those who appreciate contemplative, character-driven novels."
—*School Library Journal*

GEM

&

DIXIE

SARA ZARR

BALZER + BRAY

An Imprint of HarperCollinsPublishers

Balzer + Bray is an imprint of HarperCollins Publishers.

ISBN 978-0-06-243461-6

Typography by Brad Mead
18 19 20 21 22   PC/LSCH   10 9 8 7 6 5 4 3 2 1
❖
First paperback edition, 2018

For my big sister, Liz

With very special thanks to Jordan Brown
and Michael Bourret

WHERE ARE *we going?* Dixie would ask.

The forest, I'd say. Or, *Space.*

She never questioned me.

We need to pack survival rations, I'd tell her.

What's that?

Food and water and gum and stuff.

She'd help me make butter-and-jelly sandwiches on soft, white bread. If we had chocolate chips, we'd sprinkle those in, too, and mash the bread down hard so they wouldn't fall out. I'd lift her to the kitchen sink so she could fill a bottle with water, and I'd roll up a beach towel; then we'd put it all into the picnic basket that was really just a paper grocery bag on which I'd drawn a basket-weave pattern with a green marker—badly, crookedly.

We would put on our jackets and shoes, and I'd make her close her eyes and I'd lead her around the apartment and spin her in circles and then say:

We're here. Open your eyes.

I knew, and she knew, we weren't in space or the forest or Narnia or anywhere other than our shitty apartment. Still, when she opened her eyes, they'd go big and bright. She was good at make-believe. My favorite thing was how she always skipped into whatever fantasy place we'd gone to. As soon as her eyes were open, she'd start skipping all around the living room and up and down the hall.

We're in space, I might say. *You can't skip in space.*

I can.

Okay, but you can only skip really slow in space because there's no gravity.

Mid-skip she'd switch to slow motion and try to make her arms and legs more floaty. Then she'd get tired of it and get hot in her jacket and say it was time to go home.

No, we're not going home. We're never going home. I don't remember when I started saying that part.

She'd stop squirming. *What about Mom? And Daddy?*

We'll leave a note.

Then we'd spread the beach towel on the living room floor and if I forgot to bring crayons or markers to space I'd run into our room and get them, and we'd draw a good-bye note, our stick figures flying up to the moon and holding hands as we waved good-bye forever to our parents. Dixie liked to draw stars behind our heads like halos.

She used to play along. She used to believe everything I told her, and do anything I said.

She used to need me to take care of her, and I liked doing it. I liked doing it because, then, I thought I was the one who could. Even though nobody was taking care of me.

1.

NINE QUARTERS.

They were the last of what had been left in the jar of laundry money that Dixie and I kept in our room, the jar that had never quite lost the smell of pickle relish. I counted and recounted the quarters in my pocket with my fingertips as the lunch line moved forward, as I'd counted and recounted them through English, physiology, and government. I counted because things in my life had a way of disappearing on me, and I'd learned not to trust what I thought was there.

What was there wasn't enough—three quarters short of the cost of lunch—but I stayed in the line anyway as it moved me toward the food. Lunch roulette. Luca, the cafeteria worker on the register, might find seventy-five cents for me in his pocket. Or someone else in line might cover it, out of impatience or pity, which were just as good as kindness on a day that hungry. I hadn't eaten more than a candy bar since the potluck in my fourth-period Spanish class the day before.

Denny Miller and Adam Johnson—freshmen—stood right in front of me in the line; Tremaine Alvarado and Katy Plant, juniors like me, stood behind. Tremaine was on my PE volleyball team. She'd stare through me on the court, or jostle me while we rotated to the serve, without saying sorry or excuse me or anything else that showed she thought of me as an actual person with a name. Katy Plant thought it was funny to call me "Jim" and got other people to do it, too. I don't know what's worse—people acting like you don't have a name, or them saying it wrong on purpose. The point is I wouldn't be asking Katy or Tremaine for a handout.

Not that I wanted to ask anyone for a handout. But being hungry—I mean really hungry—had a way of erasing a lot of the embarrassment. And Denny and Adam were easy, being the kind of undersized freshmen who still looked more like seventh graders.

"Denny," I said.

Both Denny and Adam turned around. I could see

them wondering how I knew his name. I knew it because they were both listed on a program from the last band concert, and it was posted in one of the display cases outside the counseling office, under a picture of the band. I spent a lot of time there. I knew not only their names, but that Adam played clarinet and Denny played trumpet and had a solo in "Stars and Stripes Forever." They both had floppy hair and bad skin. Adam was taller, which helped me tell them apart.

"Can I borrow seventy-five cents?" I asked quietly.

"Me?" Denny pointed to himself.

"Either of you."

The line moved and the smell of ravioli and garlic bread got stronger. My stomach seemed to fold in on itself.

"I use a lunch card," Denny said.

"Yeah," Adam said. "Me too."

They turned their backs to me. Just because their parents loaded up cafeteria cards with money didn't mean they didn't also have some cash. I checked on Katy and Tremaine behind me; Katy was busy showing Tremaine something on her phone. I leaned closer to Denny. "But maybe you have some change or something?"

He drew back and shook his head. I wondered whether I'd tell Mr. Bergstrom about this in our appointment later and if I did, how I would describe it in a way that made me not look too bad.

I tried Adam. "Do you know Dixie True?"

That got his attention. "Um, yeah."

"She's in our social studies class," Denny added, facing me again. "And English."

"That's my sister." Maybe if they knew that, I would seem more interesting than weird.

They exchanged a glance.

"Really?" Denny's voice cracked on the end of the word. Adam laughed through his nose.

"Ask her next time you see her."

They wouldn't, not boys like this, zit-faced and probably still playing with action figures in secret. They might sneak looks at Dixie but they wouldn't dare say a word to her.

Denny pulled a wrinkled dollar bill from his pocket. "You can pay me back tomorrow, though, right?"

"I'll look for you," I promised, taking the money.

A couple of minutes later I had my tray of ravioli and garlic bread, a sad iceberg salad with two croutons, and a carton of milk. When I got to Luca at the register, he shook his head. "I saw that."

I handed him the bill plus eight of the quarters. He shifted on his stool, the sleeves of his green school jacket swishing against his sides while he rang me up. "If you don't have money," he said, "you should get your parents to fill out the form online so you can get free lunch. How many times I gotta tell you?"

I stared at the peeling yellow school logo over his heart. Half of a lion's mane, a third of its face. "Okay."

"'Okay,'" he said, imitating me. "You say 'okay,' then you'll be back here hustling quarters in line tomorrow, these poor little freshmen." He wasn't talking loud but not quiet, either, and I imagined Katy hearing every word.

"Those are my sister's friends," I said, and decided that's what I'd tell Mr. Bergstrom if it came up. "I'm going to pay him back."

"You always had money in the fall. What happened?"

"I saved from my job last summer. That's all gone." Since January.

His hands hovered around the register drawer for a second. Then he said, "Here's your change."

"But—" I was sure I'd given him three dollars exactly.

"Here's your *change*, Gem," he said again, putting four quarters in my palm.

"Thank you."

He waved me away, and I took my ravioli to a quiet corner to eat.

"Is that supposed to be me?"

Mr. Bergstrom had gotten a new whiteboard. He'd drawn a stick figure, falling. I knew it was falling from the way the stick arms and stick legs pointed slightly upward, like gravity was pulling on its stick middle.

"I'm not a great artist but, yes, it's meant to represent you. Here . . ." Bergstrom added some strands of hair that flew up, then capped his dry-erase marker and sat back down. "Is it at least close? Is this how you feel?"

"I don't know." In the way that she was alone, maybe, but even falling she looked more free than I felt. I got up and held my hand out for the marker. I drew a box around the falling girl. That didn't look right, either. "This is dumb." I picked up the eraser and wiped it all away.

"Maybe." He smiled. He had a good smile and a good face, and a way of looking right at me without making me feel like I was being studied in some lab. He was way better than old Mr. Skaarsgard, the school psychologist he'd replaced at the beginning of the school year. Skaarsgard would always furrow his white eyebrows at me and make me feel like nothing I said made sense. Maybe it didn't, but at least Mr. Bergstrom tried.

Normally I saw him a couple of times a week, not always on the same days, sometimes after school and sometimes during it, depending what was going on. I know it was a lot. Some kids at school could go a whole semester, even all of high school, without seeing him once. But right at the beginning of freshman year I sort of had this incident in pre-algebra, and my teacher referred me and then I was on the permanent rotation, first with Skaarsgard, now Bergstrom.

"What's the box?" he asked. "That's what it was, right?"

I shrugged.

"You feel . . ." He trailed off and I knew I was supposed to complete the sentence.

"I mean, you can't put me on there with nothing else," I said, pointing at the blank whiteboard. "You have to draw Dixie and my mom, and our apartment and school."

"Earlier, you said you felt alone."

"I do." My hands curled up on my knees, my nails pressed into my palms. This office was always hot and small. I shook my head, not knowing how to explain feeling alone but also trapped in the middle of people and places that didn't let me move or breathe.

Mr. Bergstrom had plain brown eyes, a little bit small for his face, but I could almost always see sympathy in them, like now. "It's okay, Gem," he said. "I know it's hard to put into words."

I opened my hands and took a breath.

"Do you want to update me on things with your mom?" he asked.

"They're fine."

"Fine? Last time we talked you seemed pretty worried about her. And Dixie."

Sometimes, at our appointments, I'd tell him a lot, and it felt good in the moment, finally saying the things I'd had stuck in my head all that week. But then I'd be in bed those nights, and a smothering kind of panic would settle on me that I'd said too much. Like I'd given away something I needed and couldn't get back.

"You said not to worry, so I stopped."

"Well. I think I said it wasn't your *job* to worry about your mom, it's her job to worry about you. But I know it's not that simple. Especially with Dixie." He smiled again. "And I know you didn't just *stop* worrying, Gem."

I looked at the clock. "I have to go to detention. My bus was late this morning."

He nodded. "Okay." He wheeled his chair back. "We're not scheduled again until next week, but come say hi anytime." That's how he always ended our meetings. *Come say hi anytime.* I liked knowing I could.

By the time I got home, it was twilight. Detention had made me miss my bus connection, so I'd walked, the chill and damp of Seattle a force I pressed against with every step. It was March, and things would get better and lighter soon, just not yet. Having to walk meant I missed my afternoon cigarette, too, on my bench in my park. The smoking time, which no one but me knew about, was when I didn't feel the cage or the box or whatever it was. It made space for me and my thoughts. Without it I felt like part of me was left behind, trying to catch up.

The security gate at the front of our apartment building stood ajar despite the signs all over the entryway reminding residents in capital letters to MAKE SURE the gate stayed LOCKED SECURELY because there had been CRIMINAL INCIDENTS. The dark corridor between the gate and our stairwell always scared me, especially when the gate was left open.

I pulled it closed behind me, then checked the lock. Then I checked the lock again and told myself I could stop checking. But halfway down the corridor I went back to check it again. Then, grasping the pepper spray on my key chain, I went up the three flights of stairs—past all the handwriten notes old Mrs. Wu left everywhere about noise, garbage, pets, smoking—and into our apartment.

Dixie was home. She had the TV on and a sandwich in one hand, her phone in the other, homework all over the floor where she sat. She'd changed clothes since I'd seen her at school that morning—from jeans and a hoodie to shorts over tights and a green V-neck T-shirt that showed a lot. I had on baggy jeans and a plain blue sweater that would have hidden everything if there'd been anything to hide. As usual, *she* looked like the older sister.

She looked up. "I heard you stole money from some freshman today."

Dixie had ways of knowing nearly everything that happened to me at school.

"Borrowed money," I clarified.

"Why'd you have to tell them I was your sister?"

"You *are* my sister."

"Thanks for embarrassing me."

"You're welcome."

In our bedroom I put my backpack on my pillow with the straps toward the wall. My keys went on top of the cardboard box on its side that I used as a sort of nightstand. My shoes went inside the box, laces hanging out. I hung my jacket on the closet doorknob and put on the thick socks I always wore around our apartment. Whenever Dixie saw me doing this stuff, or checking the gate lock more than twice, she'd tease me and say I had OCD. But Mr. Bergstrom asked me a bunch of questions about it and said I didn't fit the diagnosis, that it was more like I had a few rituals that helped me feel in control, and they didn't interfere with my life, and it wasn't the same thing. "Plus, from what you've told me about where you live," he'd said, "checking the gate lock sounds like plain common sense."

I confirmed one more thing—that my stash of cigarettes was still under the bed—then went back to the living room. The onion smell of Dixie's sandwich made me salivate.

"Did you get that from Napoleon?" I asked.

She chewed and stared at me like, *Obviously.* Napoleon

was the older guy who worked at the deli down the block and had a crush on Dixie—like a hundred other guys.

"Can I have some?" The ravioli from lunch seemed forever ago.

"No," she said, but held it out anyway. I sat on the floor next to her and took a bite. Then another. Roast beef. Avocado. Cheddar cheese. Thin-sliced red onion and a hard sourdough roll. It was perfect, as if all of Napoleon's craving for Dixie had been slathered onto that sandwich. I swallowed huge pieces of it, half chewed and sharp with mustard.

Dixie watched me eat. "You can finish that if you'll go down and get the laundry from the dryer."

"You did laundry? With what money?"

"Money I had."

"I'm not going down there at night," I said.

"It's not night."

She tried to take the sandwich away from me; I held it out of her reach. "It's dark, though."

"I washed some of your clothes, too, Gem. Do you want them to get stolen?" She lunged again for the sandwich.

"O-*kay*," I said. I finished it and went the five steps to the kitchenette to throw away the white paper it had been wrapped in.

"Did you see your shrink today?"

"He's not a shrink. He's just a school psychologist." I opened the fridge. There were a few stale corn tortillas, an opened bag of green beans, ketchup, and a white plastic butter dish with maybe a teaspoon of butter left, crumbs stuck all over it. Same as that morning.

"You should get him to send you to a real shrink. Say you need Adderall. You could sell it at school and then you'd have some money." I'd heard that Dixie helped some seniors sell their prescriptions at school. I didn't want to know. "I can tell you what symptoms to have," she said.

"No thanks."

I imagined going down to the laundry room. The lights could have burned out again. Sometimes there were noises that might be a zipper clanging against the dryer door, or might be rats or a creepy neighbor.

"Let's go get the laundry together," I said to Dixie.

She looked up from her homework. "You always do that."

"What?"

"'What?'" she repeated, in a bad imitation of my voice. "I already took my shoes off."

"So did I. Put them back on."

I went to the bedroom to get mine. When I came out, Dixie stood by the door forcing her flip-flops over her tights.

"You're going to fall down the stairs and die," I said as

she shuffle-walked to me.

She shrugged.

I knelt to tie my laces. "Where's Mom?"

"Out."

"I *know*. Out where?"

"Work, I guess?"

I straightened up and we faced each other.

"Do you think Napoleon would give me a sandwich?"

She laughed. "Well, you might have to flash your boobs."

"Is that what you do?"

"No! I'm joking, Gem, obviously. Do you really—" She shook her head. "You never get my jokes."

It didn't matter. I knew exactly why Dixie got sandwiches and why I wouldn't.

Dixie is pretty. No one in our family is beautiful the way movie stars are beautiful, but she's the type of girl who gets second, third, fourth looks—as many looks as people can get away with before she stares them down. She's soft in the sense of being curvy, and hard in the sense of not taking any shit. She's cute—her hair, her clothes, the faces she makes when she's surprised or mad or thinks something is funny. And intimidating. She exudes a sexuality, but in a way where it's like it's for her, not for anyone else. It started in junior high, and by the time she got to high school, people couldn't spend five minutes with Dixie before they wanted to give her things, feed her, touch her, get her to smile, be her friend, be her boyfriend. She got sandwiches, she got her cell phone bill paid, she got attention when she wanted and deflected it when she didn't.

Whereas I still hadn't figured out how to make and keep a friend.

I stared, she stared back. For her it was a game. She thought I was trying to get her to look away first. But really it was me trying to see who I was through Dixie's eyes, me wondering if she evaluated me and my face and clothes and body, the ways I made it through the world, like I evaluated hers.

Did she look for herself in me, the way I looked for myself in her?

Finally she broke, and laughed. "You're such a weirdo, Gem," she said. "You probably scared that freshman with your creepy eyes."

I didn't want her to see I couldn't take a joke, so I bugged my eyes at her to make them even creepier.

"Ew," she said with an exaggerated shudder. "Let's go downstairs before the rats come out."

2.

I WOKE up in the night, like I usually did for one reason or another—street noise or neighbor noise, a bad dream, Mom coming home from work or a night with "the girls," who, most of the time, probably weren't.

Dixie's bed was empty. She snuck out sometimes, but tonight I heard her voice with Mom's, coming from the living room. It wasn't anything out of the ordinary, them being up late together. Sometimes I could ignore them and go back to sleep. Sometimes I'd lie there with my eyes open, wishing that for once they'd check to see if I was awake. Maybe I wanted to be up talking, too.

I got out of bed and crept into the dark hall, watching

from a spot where I could see the corner of the living room. They were on the couch, facing each other. Mom's hair hung loose down her back. She'd gotten black tips on the blond.

They were eating potato chips. Dixie had one in her hand and was gesturing with it while she talked to Mom in an excited whisper. I thought I heard my name. I often had the feeling they were talking about me, especially since Dixie started high school. Before, I had my own life there without Dixie's to compare it to. Not having friends felt normal for me until I imagined it through her eyes, and I could see Mr. Bergstrom as often as I needed without anyone much noticing or caring. Now, Dixie could observe my life, judge it, and report it to Mom.

Gem is a loner.

Gem is always in the counseling office.

Gem takes money from freshmen boys so she can eat cafeteria ravioli.

These were the conversations they had in my head. I leaned farther back into the dark, listening harder.

"So I didn't change into my gym clothes. Not after he was like, 'Oh, when am I gonna see you in your shorts again?' Dick. I told Ms. Moser but she still marked it as a cut. That's why they called you."

"Gym," she'd said. Not "Gem." I scratched an itch on my arm and Dixie looked toward the hall. Mom turned around. All her silver necklaces and pendants and leather cords were draped over the scoop of her black tank top. The edge of her mermaid tattoo showed at her collarbone.

Like Dixie's, Mom's beauty wasn't model- or actress-beautiful. But still powerful. And when she and Dixie were right next to each other like that, their power doubled. In the face of it, I felt myself shrink.

"Oh, hey," Mom said. "You're up."

The smile she had for me didn't look like the one she had for Dixie. For me, she had to force it. Mr. Bergstrom once asked if this might be my imagination. If he could see it for himself, he'd know what I meant.

Mom, apologetic, held up the chip bag. "We just finished. It was only like half a bag anyway."

"Where were you?" I hadn't meant to ask, at least not before saying something else first, something that didn't sound so much like an accusation.

Dixie widened her eyes at me, annoyed. She hated when I started in on Mom. She wanted to pretend like Mom was another one of her friends, another girl with boyfriend drama and body issues and money problems who didn't need to hear shit from anyone about how she should be living her life.

Well, I didn't want to be monitoring Mom, either. But someone had to.

I stepped into the room and Mom touched the black

tips of her hair. She'd started drinking again in the last six months or so, using some. It started with her birthday in September and never stopped. *A little wine. A little pot. It's nothing.* I came closer in, to see her eyes, and tried to tell if this time it was a little wine or a little pot or both.

"I went and paid the electric bill, for one thing," she said, and looked away.

At one in the morning?

"I had to go and get a money order first," she said to Dixie. "Then the guy couldn't find our account. I gave him the number, my name, our address. . . . It was like it disappeared from the system. He had to set it up all over again, and he was a real pain in the ass about it, too." She turned to me again. "Then, like I told you or think I told you, Judy's in town. Tonight was the only night we could get together."

Dixie sat up on her knees. "They went to the Velvet," she said to me, as if I'd be excited.

Mom flashed her a look.

"Sorry," Dixie said, eyes down.

I guess I wasn't supposed to know. Like they were the sisters, me the mom.

"Only for a few hours." Mom bent over to dig around in her purse, which sagged open on the floor enough for me to see cigarettes, crumpled-up pieces of paper and dollar bills, her torn canvas wallet. "It's not the same as it used to be, that's for sure. Did you take my lip balm, Dixie?"

"No."

"Then why do I have to buy a new one every goddamn week?" She turned her purse upside-down and shook it, then spread the contents out on the carpet, sliding to the floor to hunch over mascara and pens and napkins and a couple of pieces of unopened mail.

Dixie leaned down and darted her hand into the pile for one of the envelopes. "That's for me," she said. Mom grabbed for it, but Dixie held it away and was already studying the handwriting. "It's from Dad?"

"No. I mean, I don't know. There's no return address." Mom sat back on her heels and held out her hand. The dark green polish on her fingernails was chipped to almost nothing. "Dix. Honey."

"It is from him. The postmark is Austin." Dixie pressed it to her chest. "It's addressed to *me*, Mom."

I held my breath and watched.

"Oh," Mom said with a shrug, letting her hand fall.

"Just to you?" I asked.

Dixie had backed into the corner of the couch, legs drawn up, one hand to her mouth. She had on the same polish as Mom, but hers was freshly painted.

Mom started shoving her stuff back into her purse. "Well, open it," she said. She was agitated now, more like she got after a little pot than after a little wine. Dixie knew, like I did, that Mom could turn on you fast when she was like this.

"Not right now."

"Why not? You're so fucking eager to steal it out of my purse. What do you think is in there? A check? A plane ticket? Dream on. 'Dream on, dream on,'" she sang, the refrain from an old rock song, her voice high and crazy. Definitely pot, plus maybe something stronger. I flashed on an image of her, in her bed, me trying to get her to wake up, trying to know what I should do.

Dixie's eyes met mine in search of something. Help? Sympathy? She wouldn't get either from me; she was the one who had a letter from Dad.

"Here, Gem, I got you something." Mom stumbled to her feet and handed me a matchbook from the Velvet. "Don't set anything on fire."

A matchbook. She hadn't gotten it for me. It was like how, when I was little, she used to pull random crap from her purse if we were out and I got bored and whiny. *Look what I got you, Gem!* A pen, a stick of gum, a business card. I thanked her for the matchbook anyway and scratched my nail along the edges of it.

She ran her hand through her hair and shrugged. "Ain't no thing." She tried a more genuine smile and grabbed my hand. "What's new, kiddo? Things okay at school? Still passing your classes and everything?"

This was her new game. If Dixie wasn't happy with every single thing Mom did, Mom pretended she didn't exist. Before I started to notice the moments between them that caused it, I even liked the attention. But stoned, getting-back-at-Dixie attention didn't feel much better than being completely ignored. And it had the side effect of making Dixie mad at *me*, like it was my fault.

I extracted my hand from Mom's while Dixie got up and brushed past us on her way to our room. "Whatever," she muttered.

"We need food," I told Mom.

"Do we? I feel like I just went to the store."

"Can you please just fill out that form for school? The lunch form thing?"

She rolled her eyes, massaged the back of her neck with one hand, and scooped up her purse with the other. "Gem. I am so tired. Just fill it out and I'll sign it." With Dixie gone and no one to perform for, she'd stopped pretending to care about my day or my grades or the fact that I'd hardly eaten.

"I did. But they need copies of your paychecks, or the Basic Food statements." I'd told her all this before.

Mom walked toward the kitchenette; I followed. She tossed her purse onto the small table we rarely ate at. "I don't like them having all that information about me. Anyway, isn't school food disgusting and fattening and everything? I'll get you food at the store."

"When?"

She turned around slowly. Under the kitchen light I could see her eyes were bloodshot; mascara had flaked and settled into her tiny wrinkles. Her tank top hung off one shoulder, showing a purple bra strap. Her power had dimmed. "When I get some sleep, Gem. When I get a shower and a cup of coffee. That's when. It's two in the morning. God."

I clenched my teeth. My choice was to push harder and piss her off, or back down and wind up with nothing. I had to eat. "Can I have some money?" I asked. "Like . . . three of those dollar bills?"

"What dollar bills would those be?"

"I saw them in your purse."

"Oh, you mean *my* dollar bills? The ones I earned at my *job*?"

Her job. Bartending twenty hours a week. Catching other shifts here and there.

She reached for her purse. "When are *you* getting a job again, one might ask."

"I'm trying." I'd filled out applications everywhere within a walk or a reasonable bus ride. I had no references, though, not after getting fired from the souvenir shop for always being late, which was usually the bus's fault.

"'*Do. Or do not. There is no try.*'" Yoda voice. "Okay, look, I'm going to loan you these dollar bills." She pressed a wad of money into my hand. "And I want them back in this exact condition. I *will* check every wrinkle."

I looked at the money.

"Gem, I'm kidding," she said, jostling my arm. "You're so serious. It's excruciating." With a glance toward the hall, she whispered, "Don't you wonder what's in that letter? I mean, don't you just wonder what flavor, what exact flavor, of bullshit he's selling now? I haven't heard from him in . . . Well, thank god. Not as if I want to." She fixed her eyes on me. I closed my hand around the money and lowered my arm. "What about you? Have you heard from him?"

I shook my head.

"No," she said, reaching to brush my hair out of my eyes. "I guess you wouldn't."

3.

DIXIE SLEPT through our alarms. Only the top of her head showed from under the blankets. She always slept like that. For years it was my job to get her up, get her dressed, make sure she ate breakfast, get her to school. When she was *little* little, she didn't complain, but as she got into second, third, fourth grade, we started to argue about it. She would want to wear her favorite outfit five days a week and I'd tell her she couldn't, because people would notice and tease her. She'd want candy for breakfast, she'd want to play instead of finishing schoolwork, she'd want to run ahead of me and cross the street without waiting for a green light. Around sixth grade, she decided she could do everything herself.

"You're not my mom," she'd tell me.

I had a picture in my drawer, me pushing a stroller around some city street when Dixie was a toddler and I was in maybe kindergarten, maybe first grade. Dixie's sitting there, chubby legs and curly hair. And me, pushing the stroller and wearing a grown-up's purse over my shoulder.

One morning last year I told her she had on too much makeup for junior high and she said it again—"You're not my mom"—and I took the picture out of my drawer and said, "Who's this, then? Who's pushing you around in a stroller?"

She laughed. "Someone took that picture, Gem. Probably Mom was right there, or her friend what's-her-name, Roxanne. They probably stuck a purse on you and told you to push me around because they thought it was cute."

She was probably right, but truthfully I'd never thought about who took the picture. It just existed, and me and Dix were the only ones in it. It was the image of the two of us that stuck in my head as the reality; I'd never wondered who was outside the frame.

Now, I put both hands on the lump of her and rocked it until she thrashed her arms and legs at me.

"You're going to miss the bus," I said.

"I'm not taking the bus." Her voice was muffled.

"What does Dad's letter say?"

"Nothing."

I poked her shoulder.

She threw the covers off. "Get out of my face!"

"Just tell me what it says."

"I'll tell you later," she said, and pulled the covers back up. "Leave me alone."

Mom had given me seven dollars. I doubted she'd realized she'd shoved that much at me. I also had that spare quarter from yesterday, plus the four quarters Luca had given me, which I guess technically belonged to Denny, but all together it was the most money I'd had at once since running out of what I'd saved.

I left the apartment without checking on Mom to make sure she was okay from whatever she was on last night. *Don't look and you won't see,* I reminded myself. And if I didn't see, then I didn't know, and then I wouldn't have to worry.

On the way to school I stopped by the doughnut shop that I smelled every day, and I got in line. "Apple crumb, and a glazed old-fashioned. And a milk," I said. "And a chocolate coconut," I added before the cashier rang me up.

I sat at the counter facing the street and ate all three, taking my time about it, pretending I was the kind of person who always had unlimited doughnut money and did this every day.

All morning, I looked for Dixie between classes in all the places she might be. Before third period I saw her best friend, Lia, head bent over her phone, standing outside their bio class in the black knit hat and green cowboy boots she always wore.

"Lia!"

My voice came out louder than I'd meant it to. More than one person turned to see what I was yelling about. Lia looked up, but her expression didn't change and I figured she must not recognize me. "It's Gem. Dixie's sister?"

Lia laughed. "Yeah," she said, "I know."

Then why didn't you say hi, you little snot? "Have you seen her?"

Lia's answer was to hold up her phone and show me a text she'd just gotten from Dixie.

tell mr w i'll be there in 5 mins ish

I'd be late for my next class two floors up if I waited around. "Tell her to look for me at lunch."

"When are you getting a *phone*?" Like passing on a message to Dixie was this huge pain in her ass.

"When I have a job again, I guess." I'd gotten a prepay phone when I had my job so they could call me about shift changes. Then my mom needed to borrow it for a couple of days when she couldn't pay the bill on her own phone, and after that I kept getting calls from some guy named Paul, using up my minutes looking for her. I got tired of him yelling at me and threw the phone away.

"You'll tell Dixie about lunch?" I reminded Lia.

"Yes, *okay*."

Through government class I sat in the back like always and made one hundred pen dots on a piece of notebook paper while Mr. Coates lectured on the executive branch. Ten rows down and ten across. I imagined being small, tiny enough to fit inside the field of dots, hidden.

So Dad had written to Dixie and not me. So what. The letter was probably full of lies anyway. It still ate at me; then the fact that I cared ate at me more. My father wasn't anybody I should upset myself over. He'd never upset himself over me.

I didn't see Dixie anywhere at lunch. Even after the doughnuts I was hungry. I waited until the line got short, picked up a fish sandwich and tater tots, and told Luca, "My mom got paid."

He smoothed out the bills and slid them into his drawer. "She should still fill out that form, though. She can do it online, you know."

"We don't have internet." Luca had pictures of his two little kids taped to his register. I'd noticed them before:

one girl and one boy, both with wavy black hair like his. "What are their names?" I asked, pointing.

"Jorge and Lucia."

"Lucia. After you."

"That's right. I pack them lunch every day. Food from home is better." He made disapproving eyes at my fish sandwich. *Some of us don't have food from home*, I wanted to say.

"My mom doesn't have time to cook." Time wasn't exactly the issue, but I'd rather have him think of her as a busy and broke single mom than as someone who didn't care enough about me to make sure I ate. "She gave me money for breakfast this morning, though."

"Yeah? What did you have?"

"Can I get through?" Jordan Fowler was behind me with his tray; I stepped aside. Luca rang him up.

"Doughnuts," I said, after Jordan was done.

He shook his head and looked at Jorge and Lucia.

"I'm skinny," I said. "I can eat whatever I want."

"Who cares about skinny? You need health."

Luca was only ever nice to me in his own teasing way. But him and his pictures of his kids and the way he cared more about what I ate than my own mother did—all I could see, all I could feel, was what I didn't have. I was suddenly mad at him for making lunches for his kids, mad at his kids for getting those lunches.

"If you care so much about health, maybe you shouldn't work in a school cafeteria."

"There's a salad bar," he said, pointing to it.

"You should mind your own business. Leave me alone." I walked off, with a knot in the pit of my stomach, waiting for him to call after me. *Gem! Don't be mad. I'll make you a lunch, too, sometime!* He didn't say anything, though, and I didn't look back.

Denny Miller sat by himself at a table in the corner. I went to it and put my tray down right across from his. "I have your dollar."

"Oh." He glanced over his shoulder. "That's okay."

I stacked four quarters onto his tray. "I told you I'd pay you back."

He picked them up and put them in his pocket. I sat down and started eating, and felt his stare.

"What?" I asked.

"Nothing." He picked at his food. "Just that Adam usually—"

"Is he here now?"

"No."

We ate, even though my stomach hurt over what I'd said to Luca. I put the food down on top of the knot.

"Are you really Dixie True's sister?" Denny asked, eventually.

"Yeah. Why?"

He shrugged and stared at me.

"Why?" I asked again.

His cheeks got white around the red of his zits. He picked apart his sandwich bun.

Then I saw her—we both did. She walked in, flanked by Lia and these two senior guys they hung out with. Dixie had on one of Mom's tank tops and a denim jacket over it, and a scarf. Blue tights under her short brown corduroy skirt. Denny's eyes went to me again, looking for the resemblance.

I picked up my tray and walked straight over to Dixie and her friends, who'd just sat down at a table near the door. I stood over her and said, "Hey."

"Hi?"

"Did you see Mom this morning?"

She tapped her nails on her can of soda. "Yeah. Why?"

I shrugged. "Can I . . . read it?"

"Read what?" Lia asked.

Dixie knew I meant the letter. "Not right *now*," she said, shifting her eyes to the others at the table. Then she wrinkled her nose at my half-eaten lunch. "Why don't you go eat . . . that. I'll show you at home."

"Show what?" one of the guys asked.

"Nothing," Dixie said.

"Do you have it with you?"

"God, Gem, I *told* you, not right now. Go do whatever

it is you do, your deep breathing or counting the floor tiles or whatever. I'll see you at home."

The other guy wince-laughed. "Harsh."

I turned and looked around the cafeteria with the dizzying and familiar feeling of being lost, unclaimed, and unwanted. Denny was still watching me. I raised my middle finger to him and dumped the rest of my food in the trash before walking out.

Mr. Bergstrom called me into the counseling office during PE. When I got there, he smiled like usual, and it immediately made me feel better. "Hi, Gem," he said.

"Hi."

"Sorry to make you miss class. My son has a recital right after school, so I've got to get going, but I wanted to talk to you."

"You can make me miss PE whenever you want." I lingered in the doorway, waiting to see if I was in trouble.

"Come have a seat." After I sat down, he said, "Luca mentioned that you seemed upset at lunch."

It wasn't a question, so I didn't answer. He rubbed his hand over his head, which he kept shaved. There was dirt under his nails. He'd probably been working in his yard. On the days I didn't feel like talking, he'd fill our time by telling me about his household and landscape projects.

"So, *are* you upset?" he asked.

I shrugged. "I'm not going to freak out or anything." Lose control of myself, throw something, yell. Like I'd done the time I first got sent to see Skaarsgard.

"Okay. But if Luca says something like that, I listen. Luca's a good guy. I think he kind of gets you."

I shrugged again. "What did he say?"

"He worries about how you sometimes don't have money for lunch or food from home."

"He makes lunch for his kids every day. That's really nice."

Mr. Bergstrom nodded. I thought about how to explain my anger at Luca for that, how I wished his kids would go a day knowing what it felt like without him, how at the same time I wanted to protect my mom from Luca thinking bad things about her. I worried Mr. Bergstrom would think I was a terrible person, hating someone else's little kids for having something any kid should have.

"Dixie got a letter from our dad," I finally said.

"Oh yeah?" Mr. Bergstrom leaned back and put his hands behind his head. I liked that about him, how relaxed he could be, like the only thing in the world that he had to do was listen to me.

"He only wrote to her. I didn't get anything. She won't tell me or my mom what it says. I don't think my mom was even going to give it to Dixie except it fell out of her purse when she was . . ." I didn't want to tell him she was messed up. Whenever I let something like that slip, he asked a bunch of questions I worried would get her in trouble.

He waited for more, and I didn't give more, so he asked, "What do you think is in the letter?"

"My mom says it will be bullshit."

"Are you feeling anxious about it?"

I didn't know what I was feeling, at least not in the way where I could put it into one category. He picked up his whiteboard marker and I said, "Don't draw."

"Okay," he said, laughing.

"I just want to know what it says. The letter."

"Well, there's nothing you can do about that until Dixie chooses to tell you. So maybe you can let it go until then, and whether it's something bad or good we can talk about it when we know."

He always made it sound easy.

"Meanwhile . . ." He picked his glasses up off his desk and put them on to look at his computer. "How 'bout this? Something we *can* control is I can get you on the lunch program. I think I can push the paperwork through without your mom even having to know about it."

"Really? I thought they needed her paycheck and everything."

"I'll pull a few strings."

"You don't have to."

"I know. I'll tell you a secret, though: I like pulling strings. And what's not a secret is it's faster that way."

Skaarsgard never would have pulled strings. "Thanks."

"Thank Luca." He glanced at his computer. "I'll see you in a few days?"

"Do I have to go back to PE?" It was sixth period, the end of the day.

"Nah." He wrote me a pass. He tilted his chin down when he handed it to me, to see over the tops of his glasses, and gave me the smile that made me feel like maybe in spite of Luca and Denny and Dixie's dumb friends it was okay to be me.

One of the things Mr. Bergstrom had me do when I first started seeing him was write a family history.

"What do you mean?" I'd asked. I was suspicious of him then, at first.

"You know, where your parents come from, whatever you know about your grandparents and their parents. As far back as you can."

"Why?" I already had plenty of homework.

"It might help you understand some things. It will help me, too, get an idea of how I can support you."

Support me. Skaarsgard had never said those words.

It took a long time for me to do it. My family's past isn't something I like to think about. But once I started, it poured out of me, and when I brought him pages and pages of what I'd written on note paper, I felt better, even before I read it to him.

Here's the story of my parents.

Our parents, I guess, since they're Dixie's, too. Sometimes I think of them as mine like they're different parents to me than they are to Dixie, which they kind of are. I don't have a lot of comforting memories like I guess some people do of their parents. I don't really know what I got from them that might be good. Dixie got the parts that were looks and charm. She got the confidence.

But I was there first.

My parents grew up in the eighties and nineties. They got married pretty young, in 1997. They met at a club most people don't know about called the Velvet when my mom was twenty and using a fake ID to get into bars all over Seattle. They're the type that always want to be young. For example, my dad would talk about how he'd never become like people he knew who got regular boring office jobs, and would never move to the suburbs and never turn into a paycheck-getting zombie. My mom doesn't say it in those exact words but you can tell from how she acts and dresses that she feels the same about it.

My mom got pregnant with me and they decided it was a sign to get married. They went to city hall and did the thing and changed their last names from the ones they grew up with to a new one they chose together. They named me after the diamond they couldn't afford when they got married. I was supposed to shine.

My mom was Adrienne Kostas and my dad was Russell Jacobs and they named themselves Adri and Russell True. It's pronounced like Ay-dree. When my dad needed to get on her good side, he called her "Dree." It happened a lot. But her good side got smaller and smaller until there was barely even room for herself there.

They had this dream of being in music. Not like in a band, because they didn't have that kind of talent. My mom can't even carry a tune. So their plan was to buy a club and name it Gem, after me. They'd book all their favorite bands. Then, instead of being fans who have to push their way through the crowd like everyone else, they'd be in charge of it all and get to hang out in the band dressing rooms and stuff.

Mostly they wanted to prove their parents wrong about everything. I heard that a lot when I was a kid, especially from my dad. Probably everyone tells themselves they won't be like their parents. I know

I do. But for my parents, it was more. I mean, they changed their names, so they acted really serious about it. Except the thing they did that was just like their parents was drinking. They kept trying to stop. Drugs sometimes, too. Every time one of their rock star heroes died of a drug overdose, they'd quit for a while again.

When my mom found out she was pregnant with Dixie, she stopped for a long time. But mostly, my father couldn't, and couldn't keep a job.

My father couldn't stay away from other women, either. He left us and came back a bunch of times. Mom would tell him, "Stay gone this time." Then he'd come back and she'd let him. He'd call her "Dree" and beg and say he loved her more than anything. Then, right before I started high school, my mom said he was leaving forever this time because he'd found a twenty-six-year-old version of her in Austin, Texas.

He must have known what was coming, because the week before Mom kicked him out he spent a lot of time with me and Dixie. He got us a cat and played us his old records. He took us all around the city. It was like a good-bye tour of his favorite bars and clubs. He let us skip school. He brought us to dark, dirty places where we got free Shirley Temples and peanuts. Dixie would sit up on the bar while Dad's friends or whatever they were told her how cute she was, how when she got older she'd be trouble. I guess she was around eleven then. I could already tell people liked her better than me. She was soft and bright, and I was bony and I never smiled. I guess I'm still that way. I remember sitting in the shadows trying not to touch the sticky tables, making sure I could always see the door. He made us promise not to tell Mom where we'd been.

Dixie remembers it all as an adventure, the best times we'd ever had with him. She'd tell stories to her friends about meeting the drummer from My First Crush at one of the bars. And how we named the cat Ringo Starr because Dad once interned at a studio in LA where Ringo and maybe one of the other Beatles recorded an album. After he was gone, she told her friends that Dad worked in "the music industry" in Austin and was coming back to Seattle to open a club and name it Dixie's.

I remember it more like the drummer from My First Crush throwing up in the bar halfway between the jukebox and the bathroom. And Ringo Starr disappeared off the fire escape only a few weeks after we got him.

The internship at the studio in LA was the last real job my father had in music, and it didn't even pay. I don't count playing bouncer at bars in Austin as being *in the music industry. I don't think anyone would.*

And I want to tell Dixie's friends that, actually, it was Gem. They were going to name the club Gem.

"That's all I have so far," I'd told Mr. Bergstrom after I read it out loud. "I was going to write about my grandparents next but I had to do geometry homework instead." I handed him the pages and he shuffled through them and didn't say anything. "Is that what you wanted?" I asked. "Is it okay?"

He nodded. "It's really good." He just stared at the pages and we were quiet for the longest time I remember us ever being quiet.

"It's kind of a sad story, I guess."

"Yeah," he said, and looked at me. "It kind of is."

4.

DIXIE ENDED up going home with Lia after school that day, and spent the night there. With the letter. I tried not to feel like she was punishing me somehow, like she'd made the plan with Lia just because she knew how bad I wanted to see it. I heard Mom come home in the night, but when she came to our bedroom door and said "Gem?" I pretended to be asleep.

Then it was Saturday. Dixie came home around noon. Mom was still asleep and I sat at the table doing homework. Dixie dropped the letter onto the table.

Dad's handwriting made it hard to read, his script skinny and slanted to the left.

Hey Dix,

I tried calling the last number you gave me but I guess you got a new phone or something. I hope you're still at this address because that email I had for you isn't working either. Are you trying to hide from me or something? Ha. Anyway, I've got great news at least I think it's great and it's that I'm coming back to Seattle. After I left and everything I figured I'd get a fresh start, some new—

"What does this say?" I pointed to the word and held the letter out to Dixie.

"Dreams," she said. "New dreams." She pulled something from her bag and sat across from me. It was a burrito. Before I could ask for half of it, she said, "I got it for you. I already had one."

I slid it in front of me and kept reading.

—dreams out here. But Dixie, there's no water to look at to help you think, and no real mountains, and it's hotter than goddamn hell all summer. Not to mention there are assholes everywhere you turn. So I thought I'd come back. I like my old dreams better anyway. I don't like to say this because it seems like I shouldn't have to report in to my kid, but I'm clean. Have been for a while. I want to see you and your sister but _please_ don't tell her I'm coming because she'll worry. You know how she is. I want her to see how good I'm doing before she makes a judgment on me. Also I want to surprise your mom, same deal, so let's keep this all between us.

I held it out again to point to a sentence I couldn't decipher, something about Mom. It ended with a question mark.

"I can't really read it, either," Dixie said. "But I think the point is he wants to know if she has a boyfriend."

"Does he think Mom has been sitting around at home every night, in case he came back? After all that?"

Dixie shrugged and turned away for a second, like she didn't want me to see in her face how she still believed in some fantasy version of him, of them.

Anyway, don't bother writing back because I'll be on my way. And we'll be together soon, how 'bout that? Can't wait to see my girl.

Love,
Dad

Couldn't wait to see his girl. Singular.

Dixie watched me as I skimmed back over it. _I want to see you and your sister._ I latched onto "and your sister" and wished I could have been alone with his handwriting, his words, the paper he'd touched. I wished I could have understood what I felt, what the burn in my cheeks meant, the ache in my chest. He did want to see us, he said. Us. That was the ache, I think. The burn was probably for how he hadn't even used my name, the name that had once been so important to him and my mother. Or so they'd said.

I read through it again, and in the span of a few seconds the "your sister" went from seeming like a certain kind of hope to making me feel I'd been crushed under a heavy weight. I shoved the letter back at Dixie.

"Don't be mad at *me*, Gem," she said, taking it. "At least I showed you the letter when he said not to."

That's what was supposed to substitute for feeling special, feeling loved?

"I shouldn't have let you see it," she continued. "I knew I shouldn't. I got you the burrito. I got you this." She pulled a Mars bar out of her jacket pocket and flung it on the table. "I wanted you to feel better."

I scooped up my stuff—including the food, which I'd save for dinner—and took it to our room. I dumped it on my bed without arranging anything in the usual way; it didn't seem to matter. Mom's voice came from the hall. "Dix? That you?"

"Yeah, Mom," Dixie called back.

I knelt on the floor and pulled out my box of cigarettes, got a fresh pack. I took my jacket back to where Dixie was.

"Don't tell Mom," she said.

"She already saw the letter, stupid."

"Don't tell her what it *says*. I'm serious."

Like she could keep anything from Mom. She just didn't want me to tell because *she* wanted to be the one to do it, not because she was actually going to keep Dad's secret.

"Where are you going?" she asked.

"Nowhere."

The time Mom kicked Dad out for good, Uncle Ivan, Mom's little brother, came to Seattle to help make sure it happened. Ivan's friend Greg was there, too, in case Dad didn't want to cooperate and they needed more muscle. They packed up Dad's clothes and things while Dixie and I were at school, and when we got home everything was in one big pile. Greg's back was to us while he filled a water glass from the kitchen tap. All I remember about him is the back of his head in that moment, bushy red hair around a tiny bald spot that maybe he didn't know about.

"Take Dixie into your room and do your homework," Mom said.

I looked at the pile, the edges of jeans and the corners

of T-shirts and the small wooden box that I knew was full of guitar picks and ticket stubs from all the shows he'd been to. The corner of it showed from under his beat-up leather jacket.

Dixie also spotted it. "That's Dad's special box," she said, as if only then realizing that the whole pile was Dad's, and what it meant—that after all the warnings, this was really happening.

Mom nodded and wiped at her face like there were tears there, and Dixie went and put her arms around Mom's waist. Mom said, "Gem, I asked you to take her, okay?" She pushed Ringo Starr away with her foot, not gently. Uncle Ivan leaned against the wall with the tips of his fingers in his pockets, watching.

In our room I sat on my bed and got out my homework, and Dixie lay on hers and cried. At first I tried comforting her. I said it would be okay.

"No it won't," she said.

I tried once more, and she wouldn't answer. I went to her bed and patted her back. That had worked when she was little. She would feel sad, or upset, and I would try to make her feel better. Like when she didn't get invited to a certain birthday party in second grade, or the time she lost her favorite doll on the bus. This time, she shoved me away, and I stood up, finally angry, and said, "She told him this would happen."

"You don't even care."

"He's the one who doesn't care. If he did, he'd stop."

I didn't have to explain what I meant by "stop." Just: stop.

Dixie sat up. Even with her face red and streaky and with mashed-down hair, she looked like a girl crying on TV. You wanted to put your arm around her. I wanted to. "She can't kick him out," Dixie said. "It's his apartment, too."

"Then he should come home at night. Then he shouldn't have a girlfriend. He should have a job and help pay the rent."

She pulled a pillow over her face and rocked.

"You can cry if you want," I said. "I have to do my homework." I turned my back on her.

"I hate you."

Those words, coming from Dixie, should have stopped meaning much to me, but they always hurt. I sat on my bed and worked on a math problem.

Eventually Dixie fell asleep and I went out into the hall to watch Ivan and Greg and Mom sit around the table, waiting, one or the other of them occasionally whispering something into the smoky room. They'd put Dad's stuff into boxes that someone must have gone down to the liquor store to get, and the boxes stood in a tower by the door. I scooted closer to the edge of the light and pulled my big sweatshirt over my knees.

Mostly I watched Uncle Ivan. He looked a lot like Mom only with dark hair, almost black, and hazel eyes instead of blue. He got more of the Greek-looking genes than Mom did. There was something about the way he brought his cigarette to his lips, a kind of confident and definite way, the tendons of his hands flexing, that made me wish he was there all the time.

He sensed me in the hall, glanced over, then pushed his chair away from the table. He came and stood over me, his half-smoked cigarette between his fingers. "You should probably go to bed."

I squashed myself into the carpet harder and shook my head.

He crouched down with his back against the wall. "Gem. You know what? I think this is something you shouldn't see. I think— How old are you?"

"Fourteen."

"Fourteen?" he said, incredulous. "Shit. That happened fast." He took a drag from his cigarette and looked toward where Mom sat. "I think this is something you don't want to have in your head for the rest of your life."

Already I had the tower of boxes, Dixie's crying face, all the fights and everything else that had come before. I didn't move. "What if it's the last time I see him?" I whispered.

He put his hand on the back of my head and smoothed my hair. "Yeah? What if it is? You'll be all right."

I looked at his profile to see if he meant it, or if he was saying it to me just like I had said to Dixie that it would be okay, because how could either of us know?

A little of his ash had fallen on the carpet. He rubbed it in with his thumb until it disappeared. "If it is the last time, you don't want this to be how you remember him, okay? You're going to have enough shit to shovel your way out of down the line. Trust me, I know."

"Ivan." Mom had gone to stand by the window; now she turned and gestured. "I think that's him down on the street."

Uncle Ivan squeezed my neck, and when he stood, I did, too, and went to our room; I made kissing noises so Ringo would follow me, and closed the door. But still I listened, with my ear pressed to it. In the end, Dad went quietly. He must have seen Greg and Ivan and all his stuff piled up and known there'd be no point in pushing back.

I listened for my name. For him to say my name, or Dixie's. For him to ask to say good-bye to us, demand it. I listened even as I went back to my bed, listened until I fell asleep, and when I got up in the morning, the tower of boxes, and my dad, were gone. Uncle Ivan was gone, too, back to his job and his life in Idaho.

Mom and Ivan hadn't found all Dad's things, though.

A few days later I was looking for food and saw, up on a high shelf in the kitchen, a box marked "Wedding Stuff." I wanted to see what kind of wedding stuff my parents had, but the box was full of cigarettes. Cartons of them, a brand from Mexico called Hacienda, with a man in a red serape, under a yellow sun, on each pack. I took the box to my room and put it under my bed.

Though I guess they were Dad's, they made me think of Uncle Ivan and how he'd sat with me in the hall and smoothed my hair, smoke curling around us.

I started carrying a pack of the cigarettes in my jacket pocket. Whenever I needed to—like when I felt anxious, or alone—I reached into my pocket and felt for the light, cellophane-wrapped rectangle, its exact corners and slick surface. I'd study the packaging. *Hacienda* meant something like "home." If I stared at the man in the serape long enough, I could imagine those were Uncle Ivan's eyes squinting under the sun, looking right at me, whispering the word in Spanish.

I'd learned to smoke like a real smoker. Anyone watching me light up would think I did it all the time, but I kept it to one a day, mostly in the afternoon, between school and home. I'd told Mr. Bergstrom about it, how at least at first it made me feel close to Uncle Ivan and made me think of my dad, too, like he had personally given the cigarettes to me. "Aside from the fact that you shouldn't be smoking and I wish you could maybe hold the cigarettes but not light them," Mr. Bergstrom said, "I'm glad you have the ritual." He said with that, like with all my rituals, I'd stop when I was ready.

After I read Dad's letter, I went to my spot in the tiny, neglected park near our house. My bench had a view of a tree stump that people stuffed garbage into and a sliver of the street that ran by the park. I lit a Hacienda and inhaled.

I like my old dreams better, he'd written.

What did that mean? Did it mean us, his family? One thing he'd always say to Mom when he'd screwed up was how they were meant to be, that there was no one for him but her. Or did he mean opening a club?

"GEM." I closed my eyes and saw it in neon, flashing in the Seattle mist. Inside there'd be a band on stage, my father circulating through the crowd to make sure everyone was happy. My mom . . . doing what? Working the bar? I opened my eyes and took a deep drag.

A club. What a stupid idea for people with no money, who were supposedly trying to stay clean and sober. His old dreams weren't just old, they were expired and poisonous.

I wondered about my own dreams, if I even had any. I never thought about the future. Not in the way I'd hear kids at school talk sometimes, or how people at my old job did. *I'm applying to colleges in California. I want to see London. I'm saving up for an apartment.* Those seemed like real dreams or maybe goals. The things my parents talked about sounded more like fantasies.

Anyway, I reminded myself, *even if Dad really did start a club, he'd name it after Dixie now.*

The damp extinguished my cigarette and I couldn't get it re-lit; my lighter sparked and sparked but didn't ignite. Then I remembered the book of matches Mom had given me—I'd been carrying it around as if it actually meant something.

It took me two tries to get a match lit; then I went back to my thoughts.

What he'd written about me in the letter stuck in my head like a bad song. Dixie was his girl, not me. Me, I was a judgmental worrier.

You know how she is.

Fuck him. He didn't know me and how I was.

Nobody did.

From the corner of my eye, I saw a homeless-looking man approach, half a dozen shirts and coats hanging off him, pants bagging down to his knees. People like that were always wanting to bum a smoke off me, but I didn't want to share the one thing that felt all mine. Also, why should he think I had more in the world than he did, that

I could spare anything?

I took a defiant drag, daring him to ask.

He didn't. He just sat on the other end of my bench, quiet, pulling his coats around him and staring at the stump. The fact that he didn't try to talk was almost worse than if he'd asked for something. I looked at him, hoping he'd sense it and turn, see me.

He didn't move. My eyes stung, a sensation surprising and sharp.

I finished my Hacienda and dug into my pocket. I still had a handful of change from the doughnut shop. I stood in front of the homeless man and opened my hand to offer him the quarter and two dimes in my palm. He looked up at me, his eyes blank and uncurious.

"Here," I said.

He arranged his coats but didn't make a move toward my hand.

"It's money." Maybe he was crazy. Maybe he couldn't see what I had.

"I don't need that." His voice was hoarse and thin.

The change got heavier and heavier. I couldn't spare it but I didn't want it; I wanted him to want it; I wanted to have something that someone, anyone, wanted.

He turned back to the stump. I left the change on the bench and walked away.

5.

DIXIE TOLD Mom all about the letter not long after she'd told me, just like I knew she would.

It happened Monday night. I'd been in bed for an hour without falling sleep, going over my day and all the ways I had been weird at school. Like asking Peter Chin in detention where he got his shoes. They were just sneakers but they looked new and unusual and I honestly didn't know where people shopped for things like that. He didn't even answer me.

When Dixie came home from wherever she'd been, I acted like I was asleep. Since Mom worked or went out most nights, Dixie could go anywhere she wanted without

Mom ever knowing, as long as Dixie got home first. I heard her changing for bed. She left the door open, and a little bit after that I heard the TV go on in the living room. Then I must have slept some, finally, because the next thing I heard was our front door opening, the bolt being locked, and the sound of keys dropping on the table.

"Hey, baby doll," Mom said to Dixie. She sounded tired but straight—not high, not tipsy. The rustle of a bag or something. Groceries?

I listened to their voices and could see, in my mind, the way they might be arranging themselves. Maybe Dixie lying on the couch with her feet in Mom's lap. Or maybe Dixie on the floor, Mom on the couch, rubbing Dixie's neck the way she liked.

"You do okay in classes and everything today?" Mom asked. "You went, right?"

"Yeah."

"Good. I don't love getting calls from school, so keep it together."

Dixie answered, her voice too low for me to make out.

The murmuring went on. Then Mom said, louder, "Let me see it."

A stretch of quiet.

Then Mom, even louder: "Are you *shitting* me?"

Dixie again, her voice ratcheting up, too. "Mom, just—"

"Gem! Get in here!"

I held my breath. I could have kept pretending to be asleep, but there'd have been no point because Mom was coming for me.

"Gem." Her voice got closer. Her jeans swished in the hallway. She came to my bed, the letter in her hand. "Up." She pulled the covers off me. "Your dad is trying to sell some bullshit story and we need to talk about it right now."

I followed her out to the living room. Dixie sat cross-legged on the floor, angry, looking up at me like *I'd* done something to cause all this. "What?" I said. "You're the one who showed her the letter."

"*You've* seen it, too?" Mom asked. "And didn't say anything to me? I guess I can't trust either of you girls. Good to know."

I sat across from Dixie on the floor. There was a pizza box there, too, open, with three slices left of Mom's favorite—Greek Special. I took a piece and watched Dixie. She was about to cry. I could always tell when she was about to cry.

Mom dropped onto the couch with the letter, rereading.

"This is such shit. I knew this letter would be full of it but I didn't think he was this *stupid*. He wants to 'surprise' me? What the shit kind of surprise is that? Your deadbeat ex showing up at your door with no warning.

Thanks but no thanks."

"He's clean," Dixie said.

Mom laughed. "He might have been when he wrote this. And maybe he actually is done with drugs. But he is far from clean. He's into something, I guarantee it." She dropped the letter to the floor; Dixie picked it up and glared at me, her tears spilling.

"What did *I* do?" I said.

"Nothing. Just keep shoving pizza in your face."

Mom, aggravated, said to Dixie, "Why are you such a little shit to your sister?"

That surprised Dixie and me both. Dixie looked at her lap and wiped the sleeve of her sweatshirt across her cheek.

"I'm tired of it, Dixie, okay? Give it a rest. I'm tired of every time I turn around you two are in some kind of battle." She looked from Dixie to me. "You used to get along so good. I don't know what happened and honestly it's time to grow up and out of this shit."

We *did* grow up. That was the problem.

"I'm telling you girls," she continued, "that if I had any way to reach your dad I'd call him right now and tell him to stay away from us. I don't trust him for one second. Neither should you."

"Why can't you give him a chance before . . . like . . . *judging* him?" Dixie asked.

Mom put her hands up to the sides of her head. "Dix. I know him better than you ever will. He hasn't changed. He's coming here because he wants something or because he's really fucked things up back in Austin. I promise you."

I got another piece of pizza, then Mom slid the box closer to her with her bare foot and took the last one. After a bite, she said, "He's never setting foot back in this house, and you need to both swear to me you'll keep your distance from him. He shows up, calls you, anything. You tell me. You tell me everything."

Dixie was pouting now, arms crossed, and watching us eat. "You can't keep me from seeing my own father."

"Go ahead and see him if you want. But 'keep your distance' means keep your distance. I'm saying don't trust him. Don't let him get close." She took another bite, then pointed her slice at Dixie. "You especially. You think too much of him."

"No I don't," she muttered.

Mom laughed again. "Why do you think he wrote to you and not Gem? Or me? Because he knows he's got you wrapped around his finger. Dixie, you've got stars in your eyes when it comes to him. Even worse than I did when I met him."

Dixie got up and stomped off to our room, still holding the letter.

Mom called after her, "Don't let your guard down.

He'll run you right over."

I wanted it to feel better, thinking Dad wrote to Dixie because of what Mom said and not because he loved her more. But part of me still wished it was me. I wished I was the one wrapped around his finger.

Mom lowered herself to the floor next to me. "Good pizza, right?"

I nodded.

She stretched her legs out in front of her and leaned back. "I shouldn't have spent the money. But I wanted pizza so bad. You know when you just have to have something?"

Yeah. I knew.

"You need to keep an eye out for your sister."

As if she ever had to tell me to do that. "At school she pretends like we're not even related."

Mom rubbed her temples, like our conversation was giving her a headache. "Do it anyway, Gem. Whatever you can."

6.

DIXIE HARDLY talked to me the next week. At
school it was pretty much the same as always, but then she
gave me the full silent treatment at home, too. It was a week
of Mom not going out except for work, staying straight. Like
she was trying to keep alert for Dad's arrival, and whatever it might bring with it. She bought a few groceries—a
roasted chicken, a jar of spaghetti sauce, boxes of instant
rice. She asked me about school, how my classes were. On
the weekend, she even made us breakfast. At noon, but still.

I was wary. It couldn't last.

I wanted to talk to Mr. Bergstrom about everything
going on—in our appointment or in a *Come say hi*

anytime. But in our appointment on the next Monday, words couldn't get past my throat, could barely form in my head. He tried to get me to draw on the whiteboard; I refused. He asked me if I'd found out what was in the letter and I lied, I said no.

He rocked back in his chair and waited, then rocked forward and folded his arms on his desk. "I'm kinda worried, Gem, to be honest. You're upset, and I wish you'd tell me what's up. Did your mom find out about you getting on the lunch list? Was she mad about it?"

"No."

"Did I do or say something to make you not want to trust me?"

I shook my head. He hadn't, but I knew when I heard the word that trust was something I didn't feel for anyone at that time, even the one person who might deserve it.

"Okay. I'm not going to push. That works on some people. You're not one of them. Listen, though," he said, then paused for a long time. "For the record, I *am* here and I do actually care. It's my job, but not just that."

We sat quiet. Then I asked if I could go, and he said yes but without his usual smile. I felt I'd let him down.

Through another week, I ate, at school and at home. I did my homework, I kept my side of the room neat, I smoked my Haciendas. Every day I felt sure something would happen.

And finally it did.

On the next Tuesday morning, I got called out of English. "Gem," Mrs. Cantrell said after hanging up the room phone. "They need you down in the office."

A few people looked at me, including Helena Mafi, whose seat was in front of mine. "What'd you do?" she asked.

"Nothing." I stood.

"You should probably take your stuff," Mrs. Cantrell said. There were only ten minutes left in the period. I packed my bag.

You would think he'd know better than to just show up at school, where he'd have to go through the office and bring all this attention. That was his plan, maybe, catching us by surprise, making a dramatic gesture.

His back was to the plate glass window of the office as he chatted with Ms. Behari, the attendance secretary. I saw Dixie's face before I saw his. She glowed, wide-eyed and happy, not the hard, cool Dixie she normally was at school. This was why Mom had told me to keep an eye on her. As tough as Dixie was, when it came to Dad she was a regular girl who wanted her father to love her.

So I guess it was my job to not be like her. Not be a regular girl.

I steeled myself before he turned around. I made myself

remember all the ways he'd failed, left us, messed us up. It wasn't hard.

Then he did turn, with his big smile, his Russ True charm-and-con smile. His hair had more gray than I remembered, and he wore it shorter, with a matching little gray goatee. Sunglasses resting on top of his head. He had on jeans that weren't too ratty for someone who'd never kept a job, and a Skin Yard T-shirt with a flannel over it, and he had a small brown backpack slung over one shoulder.

"Gem, baby," he said, and opened his arms.

Despite how I'd prepared myself and despite what Mom had said, despite what Dad had done and not done, despite how he'd described me in the letter in which he hadn't used my name . . . hearing it in that moment, my name on his lips and in his scratchy smoked-out voice, I went to him. And for that ten seconds or whatever it was, I held on. I pressed my face into the soft flannel. I let him put his rough cheek to mine and whisper: "See? I'm here."

When I pulled away, I saw that Mr. Bergstrom had appeared in the office. He smiled a wide, fake smile I'd never seen him use. "Is this your dad?" he asked me. He stuck out his hand. "Mike Bergstrom."

"Russ True," Dad said, shaking it, and matching his cheerfulness. "Are you the principal, or what?"

"He's the school psychologist," Dixie said.

Then Mr. Bergstrom extended his hand to Dixie. "Hi. We haven't formally met."

She shook it and we all stood there, and Dad said to Mr. Bergstrom, "Just taking my girls out a little early today to do some catching up."

"Sure, sure," Mr. Bergstrom said, with that smile. Then, "Hey, Gem, quick question if you have a sec before you go?" He motioned me toward the hall that led to the administrative offices. I didn't move. "About your schedule next week?"

I glanced at Dad, who said, "Go ahead. But make it quick, we gotta run." He threw a wink at Ms. Behari, who was not smiling.

In the hall, Mr. Bergstrom led me to an empty office and pulled the door most of the way closed. "Ms. Behari called me down as soon as he got here. What's going on?"

"Just what he said."

"You didn't tell me he was coming."

It sounded like an accusation, or at least that's how I heard it. "I have to go."

"You *don't* have to. Is this what you've been worried about?" He waited. Then: "Ms. Behari checked, and there's nothing on file that says he can't be here, but if you don't want to go or you need to tell me something else, now's the time to say it, Gem."

What I wanted to say was, Why couldn't it be true that

my father was there for exactly the reasons he said? To catch up with us, see us, because he was our father and he loved us. Why couldn't Mr. Bergstrom, who didn't know even half of everything, believe in that moment that my father had come for those simple fatherly reasons—and that I deserved that as much as anyone, as much as Dixie?

I didn't believe it, but why couldn't he?

"It's fine," I said. I looked him in the eye. "It's fine."

"Now listen," Dad said as we walked away from the school building, "Dixie told me Mom would be out all day today. The apartment should be empty now, yeah?"

It sounded like he and Dixie'd been talking since the letter had come, though I didn't know how Dad had gotten ahold of her, or her of him.

"Maybe," I said.

"She has an appointment," Dixie said to me. "Then she's taking one of Margot's early shifts and working a double."

So Mom hadn't totally been freezing Dixie out the way I'd thought, had still been telling her things. Dixie had Mom. Dixie had Dad. I stepped apart from them as we walked down the street, scared I would let my guard down if I wasn't careful, wanting a different version of us to be real.

"My idea is let's go home," Dad said. "I know it's kind

of a long walk home, but let's do it, I want to see everything. We'll go clean the place up and make it nice. We'll go shopping and fill up the fridge, the freezer, everything."

Dixie must have also told him about how things had been, our food situation. What she obviously hadn't told him was that Mom already knew he was coming back, because if she had, he wouldn't be so excited. I tried to focus on the facts, on what I could know, what was happening right now in reality. We were going home, and then to the grocery store. That's all.

"Can we get bacon?" I asked.

Dad laughed. "Sure. Whatever you want." He stopped walking and turned to me. He held his arm out. "Come here. Hey. Gem."

I went to him. The regular girl I was trying not to be went to him, while Dixie watched.

"Let me see you." He put his hands on either side of my face, his fingers gentle on the skin behind my ears. His eyes searched mine and I let them. "You've grown up. You really have."

For a few seconds it was only us standing there on the street, my father and me, people and cars around us fading away. *I was here first*, I reminded myself, and silently reminded Dixie. For a couple of years, I was the only daughter they had, the only one they loved.

Then, keeping one hand on me, he put the other on the

back of Dixie's neck, pulling her close, too. "We'll make everything perfect, then we'll wait up for Mom and surprise her. You girls need to wait up with me, okay? She'll walk in and see me and you and the clean house and the food, and she'll be happy."

"I don't think she'll be happy," I said.

He dropped his arms. "Okay," he said, nodding. "Fair enough. She won't be happy." He laughed then, like Mom being mad would be a fun adventure. "I'll get out of there fast and give her some time to warm up to the idea. I just want her to see us all together. You know there's never been anyone for me but your mom. Not in my heart."

Not in his heart. But there'd been plenty of other people in his bed, other people in his daily life in place of us.

"Is that all your stuff?" I asked.

He gripped the shoulder strap of the backpack. "Some of it. Just some clothes and business things."

"Where's the rest?"

"At a friend's. I don't have much. I'm starting over all the way." He took a deep breath of the cool air. "God-*damn* I missed this place. Don't ever go to Texas, that's my advice." We rounded the corner of our street. He put one arm around each of us. "I got some breaks. Things are coming together. This is going to be good, okay?"

We heard a shout from across the street. "Russ! Hey, Russ!"

A short guy with stringy hair and a big grin came over, dodging a car before he got to us. Dad dropped his arms and moved in front of me and Dixie in a way that seemed protective. "Do I know you?"

"Yeah, you know me, shithead," the guy said with a laugh. "It's Bongo."

After a second, Dad nodded. "Oh yeah, sure, hey."

"That's all you got for me? 'Hey'?" He glanced at us, and Dad turned and said, "Gimme a minute here." They walked down to the corner together.

"Have you told Mom he's here?" I asked Dixie while keeping one eye on Dad.

"No."

"You should. You should text her right now."

Her hand went to her pocket, where she kept her phone. "That'd only mess everything up."

"Mess what up? You seriously think his stupid plan is going to work? You know what's going to happen when she sees him in our house."

We leaned against a building, watching Dad. I checked Dixie's face. She was still trying to be happy, staring at Dad like he was some kind of rock star. But she couldn't hide her feelings, not from me. I saw the doubt already forming—about how Mom was going to take it, maybe about other things.

"That guy he's talking to," I said. "He looks like some

weed dealer or something." Or maybe Dad owed him money; Bongo wasn't grinning anymore.

"Not everything is terrible, Gem. Some things are good." Dixie folded her arms and moved away from me. "Why can't you give this one little chance to be a good thing?"

"Because I can't."

Dad came back; Bongo went the other way.

"Sorry," Dad said. "Just some loser I used to know. I wanted to make sure he knew to stay away from me and my girls."

Dixie looked at me like, *See?*

It started to drizzle. Dad laughed and looked at the sky. "Fucking Seattle, man. This is the place."

He put his arm around Dixie again; I kept myself separate for the rest of the walk home. I needed my Hacienda, and time to think. I heard Mr. Bergstrom's voice in my head. *You don't have to.* No one had a gun at my back as we walked down the street. The only gun at my back was me—not just how I'd promised to keep my eye on Dixie when it came to Dad, but also how there was a piece of me tired of trying not to be a regular girl.

So I kept walking. Dad pointed out this or that place where he used to go, asked what happened to his old favorite pizza shop, what happened to the guitar store. When we got to the front of our building, Dad looked up at it, the ugly beige, the way it was streaked with dirt. Pigeons perched on the roof and fire escapes and anywhere else they could find a square inch of space. Garbage filled the gutter and was scattered around the front gate.

"Shit," he said, letting his arm fall away from Dixie. "Did it always look like this?" The question came quiet, like he was asking himself.

"Yeah," I said. "It did."

"It's not that bad on the inside," Dixie told Dad.

He shifted his backpack to the front of him and held it close. For once the gate was locked like it was supposed to be. I opened it with my key and we went up the three flights of stairs to our unit.

"Did it always smell like this, too?" Dad asked. With each flight, his steps slowed. He stopped on the second-floor landing. Dixie stopped, too, and so did I after a couple more stairs. "What?" I asked, looking back down at them. He was as fit and wiry as he'd ever been. The stairs couldn't have been a problem.

"I don't know." He rubbed his goatee. His eyes were rimmed in red. "I didn't expect it to . . ." He could only finish that sentence with a shrug.

Dixie gave me that look again, like she was right and I was wrong, and Dad was this sensitive hero, come back to save us. For the briefest seconds of seeing him from my place on the stairs and knowing red eyes can't be faked,

I wondered if she could be right. Then a door slammed somewhere above us, and we heard footsteps coming down. Dad seemed to shake whatever he felt off, and we continued up. Dad greeted the neighbor we passed on the stairs cheerily, fake.

When we walked through the door to our apartment, he said, "Yep," nodding as he looked around, touched the wall. "I remember this." He pointed to the couch. "That's new."

The old one had been covered in tiny spots, where ash or cigarette butts had scorched the fabric before the building manager gave Mom a final warning about smoking inside.

"Used," I said.

"Used from . . ." Dixie started. "Used."

Len, she didn't say. Len, who Mom dated for a month, worked in a furniture warehouse and got us this before they broke up. We never actually saw Len himself, only heard about him from Mom. Two delivery guys from his work brought it over.

"The place doesn't actually need much cleaning," Dad decided. I don't know what he expected. That we'd been living in squalor or something? "Let's call a cab and go to the store."

7

SHOPPING WAS just like Dad promised it would be—everything we needed, anything we wanted. We stocked up on bread and apples and peanut butter, eggs and cereal, cheese, milk. Bags of chips, boxes of crackers, cans and cans of stuff—chili and soup and tuna. Also tampons and pads, and pills for cramps and headaches. Dixie slipped some makeup into the cart. I did the same with shampoo and conditioner and a serum that said it would give my limp hair more body.

Dixie smiled at me once while adding a big package of cookies to our mountain of stuff, the first of her smiles aimed at me in a week. She was practically skipping alongside the cart, skipping like she'd do when she was little, while Dad walked behind us making suggestions. "Get that cheddar popcorn, Gem, you like that."

At first I tried to let myself be happy like her. I did savor the idea of opening up the cupboard for weeks to come and always finding something to eat, and I liked it that Dad remembered my favorite foods. But the more stuff we piled into the cart, the sadder I felt. Because it wasn't how things were supposed to be. We weren't in some game show where the prize was all the groceries you wanted. Our dad buying us food shouldn't have been a special treat, it shouldn't feel like Christmas or a trip to Disneyland; we should have had it all along. There should have been child support, there should have been someone making sure we had what we needed at school. There should have been regular bedtimes and no one working nights, leaving us home all alone. We should have been getting advice—better advice than "Don't ever go to Texas."

I trailed farther and farther behind the cart and hung back while the cashier rang it all up. The total came close to four hundred dollars, and I thought Dad would freak out and tell us we had to choose stuff to put back. But he didn't. He paid in cash, and how he had that much money I didn't want to know.

We took another cab back to the apartment, with the trunk full of bags. Dixie sat between me and Dad, snuggling up to him, her hand slipped through the crook of his elbow while I leaned against the door.

They cooked dinner. Dad wanted meat loaf and macaroni and cheese, and green beans and chocolate cake. "Comfort food," he said. "Home cooking."

"Mom's a vegetarian," I reminded him as we put away groceries. As if that was the biggest problem he'd have when she got home.

"She can skip the meat loaf."

Dixie brushed past me with a can of chili in each hand. "You could try saying thanks," she muttered.

I announced that I had homework to do and left the kitchen with a jar of peanuts I'd been about to put away. I closed the door to our room and ate peanuts by the handful, barely stopping to breathe.

That was my father in there. My father.

He was the person who'd left and come back and left again and again. The person whose only reliable act was disappearing. He was the person who bought us a storeful of groceries now but also the one who'd helped keep us hungry. The one who made my mom believe we'd all be happy—they'd have the club, the dream, everything that went with it. The one who, after every screw-up, vowed to start over and never mess up again, then immediately proceeded to do exactly what he promised he wouldn't.

And he thought he could turn up, and put his arms around me and say, *Gem, baby,* and come into our house with some grand plan, filling the place up with food and making it nice. Maybe some part of me had fallen for it for a minute. Maybe a little more. But I didn't care what he said or how he looked into my eyes or how he bought us all that food, cooked us dinner like a dad on TV. I knew in my gut it was bad news, and I knew in my gut I didn't want to be in that apartment with him.

You don't have to.

I argued with Mr. Bergstrom in my head. That it wasn't so simple, especially with people around you—especially your family—saying you do have to or assuming you will.

"I bet you didn't know I could cook like this."

Dad, across from me, put a huge slab of meat loaf on my plate, next to a pile of green beans and a scoop of macaroni and cheese. The beans were from a can and the mac and cheese from a box, so really he'd only made meat loaf. Which didn't seem like that hard a dish.

But I'd had worse. Okay, I'd had much worse. It all tasted good and even though I'd already eaten half a jar of peanuts I cleared my plate in minutes, partly because I liked food and also to stuff down the dread of what would happen when Mom got home. All it would take for me to not be there when it all went down was walking out the door. But my feet were lead and I hated them.

Dad said, "I was telling Dix earlier I got a job here in Seattle."

"Already?" I asked. How long had he been in town?

"Well, I as *good* as got it. Nothing big, just working the door at Roddy's. All I gotta do is meet the manager. It doesn't pay a lot but it's not about money anyway. It's about networking." He helped himself to more meat loaf. "A lot of the connections I had aren't around anymore. Roddy's is the shit now. The Velvet's gone downhill, everyone says."

I took more food. It was surreal, the way he talked and talked as if it were normal for him to be here, and the way I sat there and listened.

"It's a stepping stone. Filling in the gap. Which I don't even really need to do." He pointed his fork at the food. "I provided, right?"

I didn't want to hear any more about his big plans and how great he was, so I said I'd do the dishes. Dad went to use the bathroom and Dixie turned on the TV and unpacked her homework. I stood in front of the sink and watched it fill with hot water, making mandarin-orange-scented steam from the new dish soap we'd gotten.

I visualized myself walking to the door, going down the stairs, out the front gate. That part I could imagine; it was what would happen after that I couldn't picture. Would it be enough to go to the park and have my cigarette and make it to tomorrow? That's how I'd been living—day to day to day. I washed plates and imagined leaving and not coming back. Then I shook my head at myself, the impossibility of it. I wasn't stupid. I knew what most girls who ran away ended up doing for money unless they had some kind of help.

While I did dishes, Dad talked his head off about Roddy's and wandered around the apartment. He'd use that job to learn everything he could about running a club now, what had changed since he'd last been in Seattle. "Bunch of hipsters these days," I heard him saying as he came back into the living room. "Not as many rockers, not as many punks, is what people say. But I know they're out there. You don't listen to any of that twee hipster shit do you, Dix?"

She said no.

"What *are* you listening to? Play me something you like. Where's the stereo?"

"We don't have one anymore," I called.

"I listen on my phone," Dixie said.

Mom had also sold off their CD collection when she needed some cash. The main noise in the apartment now was the TV.

I finished cleaning and went back out into the living room. They were on the couch together, Dad pointing to something in Dixie's homework as if he was actually help-ing. The apartment still smelled like meat loaf. It was all cozy, the way Dad wanted it to look for Mom. My stom-ach had gone into knots—with worry and also because I'd eaten way too much. I broke into a cold sweat and rushed to the bathroom, where I bent over the toilet until everything came out. I sat on the floor with my head rest-ing on the toilet seat.

It would be a good time to cry. I couldn't. I didn't. Not then and not generally. If I wasn't going to leave, there was nothing to do but hide and wait. I brushed my teeth, then went back out and announced, "I'm going to bed."

Dad looked up. "Are you kidding me?"

"I'm tired."

"She does this all the time," Dixie said, glaring. "When she doesn't want to deal with shit, she just goes to bed."

"I'm *tired*," I repeated.

"You can lie down on the floor in here and doze," Dad said. "Let's all be together when your mom walks in. United front." He threw a pillow from the couch onto the floor and pointed.

I felt my knees bend and I hated how he could do this to me in the few short hours since getting here. Make me do what I knew I didn't want to. Make me complicit.

I lay down with my back to them and looked at the TV.

8.

I WOKE up with Dixie's toes digging into my ribs and the sound of Mom's key in the door. Dad hissed, "Get up onto the couch, Gem." Before I could even move, he took a handful of my shirt and pulled me backward and up. He was strong and it scared me. When the door cracked open, the three of us were lined up on the couch, Dad right between me and Dixie. He kept his arm behind me, his fingers tucked into the waist of my jeans so if I tried to get up he could pull me back down.

Mom's face said everything. First shock, then confusion morphing into astonishment. For a second, I think, Dad thought it had worked. He must have misread her disorientation as some kind of elation at seeing us together, a family. He loosened his grip on me and smiled. But I knew better. We were screwed.

Mom threw her keys across the room. She'd probably aimed at him but the keys caught me on the shoulder. "What the *fuck*," she said.

I stood to move away from him. "He showed up at school."

It was like she didn't hear me. She pointed at Dixie. "What did I tell you?"

Dixie sprang up. Mom put her hand out, stopping her from getting too close.

"You said you wouldn't stop me from seeing him," Dixie said, pleading.

"I said keep your distance."

Dad, confused, looked at Dixie. "You told her?" Dixie's face had gone red; now Mom and Dad were both mad at her and she was going to cry. "Dix? I asked if you told her."

"Leave her alone, Russ," Mom said.

Tears spilled onto Dixie's cheeks and, despite everything, I felt bad for her. Dad got up, too, and took a few steps.

"Don't come near me," Mom said. "Asshole."

"Oh, I'm an asshole, right. I forgot. You're great and I'm an asshole." He gestured toward the kitchen. "Go look in the fridge, Adri. Go look in the cupboards."

I watched her. I wished she wasn't wearing such a short skirt. I wished she wasn't wearing such a low top. I wished she didn't have so many tattoos and such heavy eyeliner.

But she's here. That's what I told myself that moment, like I had a lot of other times when I needed to believe that in itself could be enough.

"So, what, you bought some food?" Mom said. "What happens when that's gone? Where's the four hundred dollars a month you're supposed to be sending me? Where's that?"

"Here, Dree. Look." He pulled a wad of cash out of his pocket and held it out.

Mom laughed. "Sure. Okay." She let her purse fall to the floor and kicked off her boots. She ignored Dad's outstretched hand and went to the kitchen. "Chocolate cake," she said. "Fancy."

"Thanks a lot, Dix," Dad said. "I thought you had my back."

Dixie stared at the floor. My impulse was to let her suffer—maybe the truth about who Dad was would sink in. But I was more on her side than his. "It wouldn't matter if Dixie told or not," I said to him. "Mom doesn't want you here. That's not Dixie's fault."

She glanced up at me and brushed a tear away.

"That's not the point," Dad said. "Trust is the point."

Trust. That word again, and him of all people using it.

Dixie went to him and tugged his arm. "Mom found the letter in the mail before I did. That's the only reason."

"She opened it?"

"No, but—"

"Genius, Russ," Mom called from the kitchen where she was opening and closing cupboards. "You want to keep some secret from me and you mail it right to my house."

"You didn't have to tell her what it said," Dad told Dixie. He wasn't angry like raging or anything, that wasn't his style. More trying to make her feel bad, because he knew it worked. He said, quietly and with a glance toward Mom, "I just have to know if I can trust you. It's important."

"You can," Dixie said. She'd stopped crying.

"Good, because we should be in this together. The club and everything, I want your help." He smiled at me. "Yours, too, if you want." The smile didn't fool me into thinking it made any difference to him whether he had my help or not.

Mom came back over, her phone in her hand. "I hate to interrupt your epic ideas about 'the club,' but you need to leave before I call the cops."

"Adri," he said, "take this money, okay? I'll leave. Take

this money and I'll get you more. I'll pay all of the support back."

She smiled a fuck-you kind of smile. "No thanks."

"Mom," I said. That would be a lot. Even the amount in his hand was a few hundred, maybe more.

He extended his hand to me. "Gem. You take it."

I reached for it and Mom grabbed my arm. "Don't."

"Mom, it's—"

"Trust me, Gem, that money didn't come from anywhere good." She pointed at Dixie. "You're not taking it, either. If you do, I'll find it and burn it. I'm serious."

Dad shook his head and said to Dixie, "Your mom is still so . . . Shouldn't surprise me." He put the money back in his pocket. "Guess that's my cue to leave."

"You're catching on." Mom went to the door and held it open for him. He walked right through without saying good-bye to Dixie or me. Something about him seemed different as he left, as if he was older than he'd been when he'd gotten there, or maybe just defeated.

As soon as the door closed, Mom looked from Dixie to me and said, "So. You just let him right into our house. You ate his food."

"He—"

"Like that whole conversation we had never happened." She gestured with her head toward Dixie but kept her eyes on me. "I know *she* has no backbone when it comes to him, but I expected different from you. You're going to help me clean the kitchen."

"I cleaned it already."

She breathed out a short laugh. "That's not how I mean. Dixie, go to bed."

Dixie opened her mouth, closed it, and stomped off to our room.

"Come on," Mom said to me.

I followed her. She pulled a roll of garbage bags out from under the sink and handed me one. "Hold this open for me. We'll start with what's in the fridge."

That's when I understood what she'd meant by "clean the kitchen."

"Mom," I said, trying not to let panic creep into my voice. "Let's just keep it. He owes us."

"You don't get it." She threw the cheese and the sandwich meat into the bag. The bread. The apples.

I *did* get it. How him turning up and buying food and trying to give us handfuls of cash was only a different way of lying to us. Whatever his intention, it wasn't real and it wasn't love. But the food, the money, those were real and we needed them. In that moment, though, I couldn't speak. I couldn't explain that I did understand but also that we should still keep everything. I couldn't, and I shouldn't have had to.

She scraped the leftover macaroni and cheese out of

the pot, the meat loaf out of the pan. I stood there with the garbage bag trying to think of ways to talk her out of it that wouldn't make her mad. Like, *Why don't we go ahead and save the canned food for an emergency?* Or, *Maybe you'll change your mind in the morning.* She should sleep on it, I could say.

But it was all garbage to her and she wouldn't stop until we were back to nothing.

She filled the bag until it was too heavy to hold. "Get me another one," she said. I didn't move. "Fine," she said, "I'll get it myself." First, though, she took the full bag and opened the back door. I heard it slide down the chute and crash into the big garbage can at the bottom.

I found some words. "You don't have to eat any of it, Mom. I'll . . . I'll take it to a food bank or something tomorrow, okay? We could give it to Mrs. Wu, leave it outside her door." I could fit a lot of cans under my bed.

Another bag went down the chute.

I held the roll of garbage bags away from her, hoping to salvage what was left.

I can still see exactly how she looked, small and frail and afraid. The way she blinked with something like surprise as she looked around the kitchen, probably already regretting throwing the food away. Sometimes, when I remember it, I add a moment, in my imagination, where I step toward her and put my arms around her and tell her

I'm sorry and I wish everything was different.

I didn't do any of that, though. I stood still and mute while she bundled herself in her own arms, shivering from the draft the back door had let in, and said, "You have to understand, Gem. I used to love him so much. We were destiny, made for each other. I would have loved him forever. He fucked it up. I could have dealt with the drugs. Together we could have dealt with it. But he became this . . . liar. He wasn't like that when I met him, he wasn't."

Her voice got quieter and her arms dropped.

"The women, Gem. I hope you never know what that feels like. It feels like shit," she continued. "You wonder if anything was ever true. You wonder if you're the stupidest woman who ever lived. It makes you crazy. It puts you on the floor tearing your hair out wondering if you could have done something. Like *you're* the one who messed up when it's them you should be blaming all along."

I remembered how it was sometimes when we were little, before he left for good, Mom in bed for days, clean and sober but wrecked by a broken heart and cursing him.

And I understood being made to feel guilty for things that weren't your fault.

"Now he's going to come back?" She squatted down to pick up a bag of salad that had fallen to the floor. "He thinks walking in here like fucking Santa Claus with presents and toys is going to make me look bad and him look good?"

"It doesn't," I said. "It doesn't make him look good."

"Dixie believes in that shit, Gem. She believes him."

"I don't," I assured her.

She continued as if she hadn't heard me. "I can see in her face. She thinks he's coming through."

"He's not."

"Yeah, well, you're the one who let him in today. You're older, Gem. You were supposed to keep an eye out for her."

My fault, was what she was saying.

She straightened her skirt and wiped her fingers under her eyes to clear the streaked mascara there. I followed her to the living room. She dug in her purse and came up with some money. "It's only ten bucks. But it's enough for lunch for both of you tomorrow, right?"

I nodded and took it. It wasn't the time to say I'd gotten on the lunch program or explain again how Dixie always figured out her own way to pay for it.

"I can take care of you." Tears had returned to her voice. She held on to my arm like she needed more than anything in the world for me to believe what she'd just said.

I didn't, but I told her, "I know you can."

This look crossed her face and then she wasn't there.

She'd gone somewhere else in her head. She let go of my arm and said, "I'm going to my room. I need to think I need space. I need to . . . Just leave me alone in there. Okay? Let me disappear for a while."

Let me disappear.

I knew what that meant.

I was tired and empty. Tired of trying to stop her from her bad decisions. Empty of any love, any sympathy. She'd basically announced to me that she was going to use, and I didn't feel anything.

"Good night, Mom."

She brushed past me and I watched her go to her room. She got smaller and smaller. She shrank to nothing.

9.

DIXIE WAS sitting up on her bed, her face illuminated by the light of her phone, which she held in one hand, like she was waiting for it to do something. Tissues were piled around her. I wished I could cry like that, let it all out anytime I needed to. I pictured my own tears, the ones that never came out, turning into little pebbles and piling up inside me. I pictured them filling my fingertips and feet and stomach, weighing me down.

I needed my Hacienda. I put on my jacket and felt for the pack, and slipped my feet into my shoes.

"Where are you going?" Dixie asked quietly, and put her phone facedown on the bed.

"Fire escape."

She sniffled, "Can I come?" Her voice was small.

"There aren't any lights in the alley."

"So?"

"You used to be afraid of the dark." Of the dark, of strange noises and shadows, of the hours we had alone together after school when Mom worked days and Dad was doing whatever and we were tired of the runaway game. That stuff scared me, too, but I pretended it didn't, for her. I'd tell her: *Draw a dinosaur for me. Draw a princess.*

"Every kid is afraid of the dark," she said.

"Maybe."

We climbed out. The metal grating was wet from when it had rained earlier. I reached back into the window and pulled my blanket off the bed for us to sit on. I touched the cigarettes in my pocket and knew that if I smoked now, the secret of it, the privacy, would be gone forever. The trade-off seemed worth it to show Dixie that I wasn't exactly what she thought I was. To be the big sister again.

I withdrew my hand from my pocket and held up the pack. "Want one?"

Her eyes widened.

"What?" I asked, pretending it was no big deal.

"To quote Mom," she said, "'are you *shitting* me?'"

I didn't move, and a small eruption of laughter came

out of Dixie before she put her hand over her mouth. I had to laugh, too. Her imitation of Mom was perfect, and I could imagine how strange me smoking looked to her. Then our hands shook with trying not to laugh too loud as we lit our cigarettes—that crazy kind of laughing that feels almost the same as crying.

From the way she inhaled I could tell it wasn't her first; I wasn't introducing her to anything.

"Mom threw away the food," I told her after we'd each taken a couple of drags.

"What food?"

"The *food*."

"Like, the leftovers? From dinner?"

I blew smoke into the air, watching it curl and wind through the fire-escape grating. She had such faith in Mom. "All of it, Dixie."

I felt her letting it sink in.

"I tried to stop her."

A man was looking through a Dumpster in our alley. We stayed quiet until he'd gone; then Dixie flicked her half-smoked cigarette off the fire escape like she'd done it a hundred times before. She shivered.

"Is she still up?" she asked.

"She went to her room." I stubbed my own cigarette out. "She said to leave her alone."

"I want to get the stuff out of the bathroom before she finds that, too."

She meant the tampons and shampoo and everything. When she turned to climb back through, I figured that was it, our moment together was over. But she glanced over her shoulder and said, "Come on."

We crept down the hall. The bathroom light was on, the door ajar. We waited a second to make sure Mom wasn't in there; then I went in, knelt on the floor, and opened the cabinet under the sink, pulling out the boxes of pads and tampons, and the shampoo with its matching conditioner that had the words "Hydration Balance Shine" lettered onto the bottles. A jar of hair cream Dixie had gotten, the serum I was going to try. The razors. Dixie found a plastic bag to put it all into.

Back out in the hall, I couldn't help but notice how quiet it was. Dixie felt it, too. She handed me the bag of our stuff and went to Mom's door, nudging it open.

"Dixie," I whispered. "Let's just go to bed."

Mom lay on the bed in her clothes, blankets half pulled over her, and from the position she was in you could tell something wasn't right. Her body was too loose. Dixie went farther in. "Mom?"

"She said she wanted to disappear."

Dixie knew what that meant as well as I did. But she

still kept walking. I stood frozen in the doorway.

"I just want to make sure she's breathing and everything," she said.

I watched as she tried to get some response out of Mom. For years it had always been me trying to wake Mom while Dixie hung back. I watched as if watching myself, trying to remember the girl I'd been, the girls we both were, how small we must have been, and how scared.

Now, Mom mumbled something unintelligible, waved one of her arms as if shooing Dixie away. "What did you take, Mom?" Dixie asked. "Mom?"

I took a step closer.

"She's breathing okay," Dixie said to me. "Come help me look around."

I finally went in. The room smelled stale and was colder than ours. Mom had her window open about an inch. We silently searched, moving aside clothes and jewelry and makeup. We opened drawers and all the little decorative boxes Mom kept on her dresser and bedside tables. Dixie found it on the bookcase by the window—the chalky residue of something.

"What is it?" I asked.

"Probably oxy. Maybe mixed with something else."

She kept searching. She reached her hand under the mattress and felt around until she pulled out a handful of tiny plastic bags. "These are old ones, empty."

"How do you know what it was?"

After a pause Dixie said, "Because I got it for her. At school."

She pulled the blankets up around Mom's shoulders, then walked out. I followed, not as shocked as I probably should have been. Nothing about our family surprised me, I realized. It was following exactly the path it had been on for a long time.

When we got to our room, Dixie sat on her bed. "She'll be okay. I get her stuff sometimes. Don't yell at me, Gem."

"I wasn't going to." I flipped on the overhead light. One of the two bulbs flickered, then died. "She hasn't been in there that long. It works that fast?"

"If you snort it. And maybe she was already on something when she got home from work. I didn't think—"

"I don't care," I said. And I didn't. I didn't care.

Our room looked dingy and sad in the low light, more so than usual. And it smelled a little bit like smoke. I smelled like smoke, too—smoke and sweat. It was only a few hours before dawn, then school. "I'm taking a shower."

"Now?" Dixie asked.

"Yeah." I carried the plastic bag of our stuff into the bathroom.

The new shampoo smelled like coconut. I used it all over my body. I shaved my legs with a fresh razor. I massaged the conditioner into my hair and stayed in the shower until the hot water ran out, then sat on the closed toilet in the steam for a long time, working the serum through my split ends, my arms heavy, full of little pebbles.

Dixie was on her bed, on her back, her arm crossed over her face. "I'm awake," she said without moving. There were more tissues piled up and tears in her voice when she said, "I checked on Mom again. She's the same."

"I don't care," I repeated. I let my towel drop to the floor and dressed for school, limbs heavy, moving in slow motion. "You're the one who's worried. Or do you feel guilty?"

She sat up, and her face was puffy from crying but also glowing, like crying made her even more herself, her eyes brighter, her lips redder. "She made it sound like no big deal, Gem. She said her shoulder hurt from carrying trays of drinks and whatever, and she just didn't have time to go to the doctor, and she knew there was all kinds of stuff to get at school. She didn't beg or anything. She didn't seem like . . . you know, *desperate*. She seemed—"

"I said I don't care."

She fell back over onto her side. "Dad was such a dick to me."

"Not just to you." I got down on the floor with the bag of shampoo and stuff. "I'm hiding this under the bed."

There was room for it in the box with the cartons of Haciendas. I reached under to drag it out, and the tips of my fingers felt something else there. I couldn't quite reach it, so I lay down on the floor to get more of my arm under, and pulled it out.

It took me just a second to recognize the brown backpack Dad had been carrying around.

Feeling suddenly sharp and awake, I looked at Dixie. "Did you put this under my bed?"

She rolled over to the edge of the bed to see. "No."

"Did you see *him* put it there?"

"No!" She sat up, indignant.

"Well, when did he, if you didn't know? Did he come in here when I was doing the dishes?"

"I don't *know*, Gem. I guess he could have?"

I looked at the worn brown canvas, imagining Dad in our room, rushing around looking for a place to stash the bag. Mom's words repeated in my head: *He's into something, I guarantee it.* Drugs, probably. It would make sense, that his big plan for success had been to bring in a stash from the border and sell it in Seattle. Just another unsurprising development in the mess that was our lives. I reached for the zipper.

Dixie was up and grabbed the backpack away. "Wait. I should call Dad. Let me call him."

For a second I doubted her claim that she didn't know

any more about it than I did, especially having just found out she'd been getting pills for Mom. Maybe Dad was going to get her to deal at school, maybe that's what he meant when he'd said how important it was for him to be able to trust her. Would he do that? *Yes,* I thought. *He would.*

I watched her face and she didn't avoid my eyes, which made me think she really didn't know. "We're opening it first," I said. "And if it's drugs, we're calling the police. Then you can call him all you want."

"The *police*, Gem? With Mom like she is right now? I could get in real trouble if they found out what I did."

I didn't want anyone to get in trouble, not that kind of trouble. "I just want Dad to go away," I said.

That wasn't it exactly. I wanted my father. But I wanted him to be a different person than he was.

Dixie cradled the bag in her arms like it was a baby. "He's probably—"

"Fine," I said, stopping her before she could voice another excuse for him. "Call and ask him what's in the bag. You think he's that great? Ask. Ask him if everything today—buying us groceries, cooking dinner—was all so he could stash this here without us noticing." She held the bag against her chest. Her phone was on the floor by the bed. I picked it up. "Or I can call him and ask."

Dixie slowly lowered the bag and slid to the floor with

it in her lap. She looked at it a few seconds, then passed it to me. "You open it. I don't want him getting mad at me."

Maybe it was her being younger that made her care so much what he thought. Fourteen—even almost fifteen— is pretty far from seventeen when it comes down to it. Or maybe it was that she had better memories of him than I did, a different picture of him, since he'd always paid her more attention. Unlike me, she still had something left to lose.

I can remember the sound the zipper made. It snagged a couple of times; then I got the bag open in three short bursts and peered inside.

"What is it?" Dixie asked.

I reached my hand in to widen the opening, to see how much was in there.

Then I stared at Dixie and dumped the contents of the backpack onto our floor.

Her mouth fell open. She got up onto her knees and bent over it.

"Holy shit. Holy fucking shit."

EVERYONE PLAYS the runaway game when they're little. Maybe they run away in the house, like we did, only pretending to be gone. Or if they're in an okay neighborhood, they might run away down the street, to a park or a neighbor's house. But it's a game you grow out of. Most kids, when they get older, realize they have things pretty good, that their parents love them and that not getting dessert every night or having to share their toys isn't the end of the world.

Besides, those who really do want to leave, who need to, have to figure things out. Like how they'll survive. They need a plan, they need help.

Or they need money.

"How much do you think this is?" Dixie asked as she stared at the cash on our bedroom floor.

Stacks and stacks of it. It wasn't all neat and organized and new looking, like on TV. Some of it was bundled, some of it loose and crumpled. There were ones, and there were twenties. There were fives, lots of fives. Literally at our feet.

I picked up a bundle and flipped through it. "These are all fifties." I put that one down and picked up another. "Tens."

Having it all spread out on the floor made me nervous; with our luck, I could imagine Mom miraculously coming out of her drug stupor and walking in on us, or Dad turning up with an apartment key that he'd somehow gotten. I started to put it all back into the bag.

"Wait," Dixie said, grasping at the money. "I want to count it."

I sat back on my heels. I made my thoughts slow down, I made myself breathe like Mr. Bergstrom taught me. What were the facts? What was reality? A pile of money. That Dad had hidden in our room. Another reality was Dixie, and that she still felt loyal to him and could pick up her phone any second and call to tell him we'd found the money. But she also still felt loyal to Mom and might tell *her*.

And another reality, one that I pushed to the side for later, was what a person—a person like me—could do with that money.

My goal, my only goal right then, was to keep Dixie from telling either of our parents what we'd found.

"Weren't you going to call Dad?" I asked her carefully. "You could ask him how much it is."

She drew her hands back. Her phone was right next to her on the floor. I held back the impulse to grab it, knowing that would backfire.

"Or," I said, "do you want to wait until Mom wakes up and ask *her* what to do? Remember how she said she'd burn any money we got from Dad?"

"She wouldn't."

"You didn't see her, Dixie, throwing bags full of food down the garbage chute. But go ahead. I'm sure the mom that got you to buy drugs for her will give great advice."

Dixie's expression clouded. "Why are you being like this?"

I stood. "I'm being like this because after everything we've been through you still act like they're normal parents who are capable of doing normal parent things like solving problems and taking care of us. I mean, look at only everything that happened *today*, never mind our whole lives." I pointed to the money. "Think about it, Dixie. What kind of a father would use his kids' room to stash drug money or whatever it is?"

"You think it's drug money?"

"Or whatever it is. You think he earned this? At a job?"

She halfheartedly straightened a stack of the bills. "I'm sure he has an explanation."

"I'm sure he does."

I sat on my bed, barely breathing now, and she stayed on the floor between the phone and the money, staring blankly, looking at neither. After a few seconds she reached over for the backpack and slowly started putting the money into it. "Okay. So what do we do?"

I exhaled. "Let me think."

The window was still open. Heavy mist had coated the glass in droplets. Sounds from the street—cars, mostly, and a few voices—floated up to me. I'd done it, kept Dixie from calling him, gotten her to look to me for the answers like she did when she was six, eight. Now, I wanted to figure out what Dad would do next, how much time we'd have to come up with a plan. But I was exhausted and cold and the only thoughts I could manage were about myself.

"It's a shitload of money, Gem."

"I know." I stared at the bag and thought about what I would have done if I'd been all alone when I found it. "Let's put it back under the bed for now. Like it was. And don't say anything to Dad."

She'd drawn her knees to her chest. "Maybe he wants to give it to us. Maybe he did earn it, Gem. Maybe he wants to take care of us. This must have been what he used to buy us groceries, right?"

I saw the little girl she'd been, saw it in her face, but more in what she was saying and in her voice—the tired, desperate hope of having to convince yourself of something that should be unquestionable.

"Maybe," I said, slipping easily back into the role of big sister, comforter. "For now, don't say anything." I put the bag back under the bed, right where it had been.

"I won't." She got up and crawled under her covers.

I turned off the light and lay on top of my bed. We had a couple of hours before we'd have to leave for school. Despite how exhausted I was, I decided not to let myself sleep. I still had to make sure Dixie didn't call him, or text him, or go to Mom. No matter what my sister promised, or how tough she thought she was, how grown-up and world-wise and smart, when it came to them she was more fragile than I'd ever been, or would ever let myself be.

11.

I SKIMMED the dense blocks of text in *The Grapes of Wrath*, hoping to get something down about it in my overdue reading journal before class started. Focus never came easily for me, and that book, full of dust and farms and a hundred different characters, was especially hard to follow. But Mr. Bergstrom often reminded me how important it was to graduate, so I tried.

My feet rested on my backpack under my desk; I tapped my pen against my notebook. I wrote two sentences about how confusing the story was, then got distracted by wondering if Mom had gotten up yet. She'd still been in bed when I left, and Dixie had been in the shower.

Helena Mafi came in and hung her jacket on the back of her chair. I wouldn't say we were friends, but if I had to stare at the back of someone's head for an hour every day, hers was better than most. Her hair was black and always shiny, with a slight wave to it.

"Hey," I said.

She turned, with raised eyebrows.

"Did you do the reading?" I asked, holding up the book.

"Yeah." She sat down and got out her own copy.

Mrs. Cantrell had gone to the door to call in stragglers.

"What happens?" I asked Helena.

"It's a little complicated to explain in two seconds."

"Where are we even supposed to be? In the reading?"

Flipping pages, I jiggled my leg up and down. What if Dixie was telling Mom about the money right now? I knew it was a risk to leave her there, but I hadn't wanted to be late, hadn't wanted to do anything that would call attention to me, and most of all hadn't wanted to have to see Mom, myself, before I got out.

"Here," Helena said, annoyed. She took my book and found the page. "Your leg is bumping my chair." She handed the book back to me. "It's annoying."

I stopped. "Sorry." I tried three deep breaths. It helped slightly. I read the page Helena opened to. There were children in this chapter, children barefoot—in dust, always dust—and watching a man eat a sandwich, wanting it.

I tapped Helena's shoulder.

"Yes?"

"I'm really sorry," I whispered. Cantrell had started class. "About jiggling your chair."

"I know. You just said that."

"I am." I wanted her to remember me in a nice way.

She tilted her head toward me. Her hair touched my desk. "It's *okay*, Gem. It's not a big deal."

The ragged children on the page ate fried dough and listened to poor men talk about being poor and how they wanted to kill the other men, who were making them poor.

I pushed my feet against my backpack, reassuring myself it was still there.

On my way to lunch I stopped by Mr. Bergstrom's office. Mostly I wanted to show him everything was fine, like I'd said when Dad came. And to see his face again. His door was open but he was on the phone. He covered the mouthpiece with one hand and said, "Hey, Gem, if you come back later, I've got some time."

"It's okay." I stood there while he listened to whoever was on the phone, cradling it against his shoulder. I imagined never coming into his office again, never sitting down across from him.

He looked at me over his glasses. "Hang on, sorry," he said to the person on the phone. Then, to me, "I need to talk to this guy about something I should keep confidential."

"Oh, okay."

"Come back after lunch?"

"I can't . . . I shouldn't miss class."

"Not even PE?" He smiled that smile, the one that made me think I could be all right.

"Not today." I left his office, waving a small good-bye. Maybe if he hadn't been on the phone, I would have told him more, asked him a question or something, but it didn't work out that way.

In the cafeteria, I picked up a brownie along with a turkey burger. I held a five-dollar bill in my hand. When I got to Luca, he said, "Burger's on the program, but I do gotta charge you for the brownie."

"I know," I said. I gave him the money.

"You seem better today. You're not yelling at me."

"I didn't yell at you." My face got warm. Like with Helena, I wanted him to remember me well.

"Okay, your voice didn't yell but your words did." He caught my eye while making change and smiled. "Hey, don't get upset. I'm kidding you, sort of. Don't worry."

"Thanks for talking to Mr. Bergstrom. I know you didn't have to do that."

He waved my thanks away. "No problem."

I pushed the change back at him. "Here."

He laughed. "I can't take that."

"Give it to Lucia." I pointed to the pictures of his kids taped to the register.

"I can't." He put the change on my tray. "You have a good afternoon, Gem."

I looked around the cafeteria, nervous. Every minute that passed was a minute Dad could be back at the apartment, looking for what he'd left, a minute Dixie could be calling him, a minute she could be talking to Mom. Still, I didn't want to rush anything. And I wasn't sure, not completely, of what I was doing or going to do.

I wanted to see Dixie first.

I took my tray over to Denny and Adam's table, empty except for them, and sat right next to Denny and across from Adam with my backpack on. I picked up a dollar from the change Luca wouldn't take and held it out to Denny. "Thanks again."

"You already paid me back."

I pretended I'd forgotten, shrugging the shrug of people who are never short of dollar bills to see what it felt like. "Do you want a dollar?" I asked Adam.

"Um, no." He glanced at Denny and then cleared his throat. "Dude, let's go sit with Martin and those guys."

Denny's zits got extra red. I met his eyes and ate my

turkey burger. He muttered something to Adam that I couldn't hear. Adam had put one hand on either side of his tray and made like he was going to stand up to go when we all heard my name shouted across the cafeteria.

"Gem!"

Dixie was striding over, her phone in her hand. Something had happened, I could tell. Maybe I'd already waited too long.

"That's my sister," I told Adam.

"Yeah, you said." He stared at Dixie, at the way her body moved every time she put a foot down on the linoleum—her unique tough-soft bounce. His neck flushed.

"What are you looking at, *Johnson*?" Dixie said when she got to the table. Adam got up with his tray and disappeared. Then Dixie widened her eyes at Denny like, *Go away*, and he left, too.

Dixie stuck her phone in front of my face. There was a text from Dad.

> **hey I left something at the apartment and mom won't let me in. text me when you get home and coast is clear so i can pick up**

"What should I say?" she asked, sitting next to me. "I'll just say okay and pretend I don't know, right? Like we said?"

I took a bite of my brownie. It was gluey and too sweet. What I'd eaten of the burger was already cement in my stomach. Sweat trickled down my back even though the cafeteria was chilly, as usual.

"Did you tell Mom?"

She frowned. "No! No."

I believed her. Because her doing that—showing me the text right away and asking what she should do—it told me that things were different now. And if they were, if she looked to me to be the big sister again the way I thought I wanted her to, then I'd have to consider that before deciding exactly how to handle the next moment, and the one after that.

"Ask him what it is," I said. I wanted to see how he'd lie, and I wanted her to see it. To prove my point one more time.

She hovered her thumbs over her phone, then typed. In a few seconds, his reply came.

just some business papers and stuff

Dixie showed me.

"I told you," I said quietly.

Then he added:

it's important tho. how soon can i get? can you leave school early?

"He probably just doesn't want to say anything about it over text," Dixie said, but without the urgent defensiveness she'd had the night before.

"Dixie . . . here." I reached for the phone; she pulled it

back. "Fine, you do it," I said. "Call him. Ask."

The warning bell rang. People began to get up and file out of the cafeteria.

Dixie stared at her phone a few seconds, then sent another text. "I asked if I could bring it to him. Instead of him picking it up. I asked him where in the house he left it."

The cafeteria was almost empty, and the final bell rang. I stood with my tray, aware of the lumpy lightness of my backpack. "He's going to lie," I said. "He won't want you to touch it or see it. He won't want you to know what it is."

Her phone buzzed and she hunched away from me so I wouldn't try to read over her shoulder. I threw out what was left of my brownie, bused my tray. "What did he say?" I asked.

"Nothing." She shoved her phone into her pocket and stood, heading for the door.

I followed her. "He lied."

"It wasn't even him." She walked faster and then threw her body against the cafeteria door where it exited to a courtyard with picnic tables.

I tried to catch up with her, worried she'd buckle and tell him we'd found it. I got close enough to grab her jacket. I yanked it off one of her shoulders and took the phone out of her pocket before she could stop me.

"Don't, Gem!" She flailed and grasped but I saw the message anyway.

maybe I didn't leave it there after all. need to check around here first. forget it and never mind ok? i'll get in touch in couple days after mom calms down lol

She succeeded in getting the phone away from me. "Don't. Do that." Her voice shook. She straightened her jacket. "If Mom hadn't gone so crazy on him last night, he probably would have explained everything."

"We were with him for however many hours from the time he got to school yesterday. He could have explained it anytime."

"He wanted Mom to be there."

"Dixie, he—" I stopped myself. It didn't matter. None of this mess with Dad mattered. I didn't even care how he got the money or why he got it or what he planned to do with it, wrong or right, illegal or legit. I didn't care about any of that.

She was waiting for me. Waiting for me to tell her what we should do, like when I'd have the paper bag packed full of picnic stuff for our games. Survival rations.

Where are we going? she used to ask.

And I was the one to tell her.

I slipped my backpack off, checked to make sure no

one was around, then stepped closer to her. "Look," I said, and unzipped the backpack just enough to show her what was inside.

She peered in, then moved away from me, glancing over her shoulder and all around. "Why'd you bring that to school! You said we were putting it back under the bed! The bag was there this morning when I looked. You said—"

"Come with me." I zipped the bag up, slung it over my shoulder.

"Wait," she said. "Come with you where?"

The assistant principal would come through on her postlunch sweep of the campus any minute. I didn't have time to outline to Dixie something she should already understand. I crossed the courtyard, away from her and toward where the fence opened to the street, my heart in my throat, worried I'd made the wrong decision. If I'd gone with my other plan, I would have had a head start and it would have been hours before she, or anyone, figured out what I'd done.

"Where are you going?" Dixie called after me.

"I don't know." I kept walking. I needed to get off the school grounds.

"Gem, wait. *Wait!*"

A bus to downtown was a block away, headed toward the stop in front of the school. I turned to Dixie. "Let's get on this bus," I said. "Let's just get on this bus and . . . talk."

She looked angry, betrayed, "Why should I?"

Because Mom said I had to look out for you; because of the picture in my bag of us, you in the stroller, me pushing you along; because, right now, this is the chance.

I glanced at the approaching bus.

And because if you don't, you're going to call Dad and tell him what I'm doing.

"You trust Dad more than you trust me?" I asked. "Which of us was always there for you?" The bus heaved to a stop in front of us. "Get off at the next stop if you want. I just want to talk to you."

The doors sighed open. I stepped on and tried not to move too quickly, act too desperate, be afraid. Dixie hesitated long enough that the driver leaned over and said, "I'm on a schedule, hon."

Dixie climbed on after me. The doors hissed closed. We lurched forward.

WE SAT in the back. Dixie didn't get off at the next stop, or the next, or the next, but she refused to look at me. There were only a few other people on the bus, all clustered in the front.

"Okay, so talk," Dixie finally said.

I put my hand in my pocket, felt for the edges of my pack of Haciendas. "If Dad doesn't check back on the apartment for a couple of days, like he said, then we have some time."

"Some time for what?" she muttered to the window.

"Time. Time to decide, or . . . whatever we want."

She turned to me. "Decide? We already decided. We

decided to leave it where it was and pretend we hadn't found it."

"I said 'for now.' That's what I said."

After a second she said, "You're really stupid, Gem. You know that, right?"

Stupid would have been if I'd left the money at home with Dixie when I'd gone to school that morning.

"I mean, you think you're going to start some new life and Dad'll just let you take it and you'll live happily ever after?"

"I don't think that." Not the 'happily ever after' part. I hadn't thought that far ahead.

She looked away again. "And what about Mom?"

I didn't want to think about Mom or talk about Mom or worry about Mom. Mom should have been the one worrying about us, like Mr. Bergstrom had been trying to tell me, and I didn't fully get it until I watched her throw away the food, until I saw her disappear on us once again when we needed her most.

"Mom isn't going to change."

"That's not what I mean," she said, though she didn't argue. "I mean, you can't *go* anywhere. She'll freak out if you don't come home. She'll call the cops."

"You actually think that? I don't think she'd even notice for a while."

Dixie laughed. "I know she's not perfect, but she'd

notice if you weren't there, Gem."

"Maybe."

"Definitely." She slid the bus window open a couple of inches and put her face near where the air came in.

"Can you text her for me?" I asked. "Tell her I'm staying with a friend tonight?"

"What friend?"

"Say Helena. Say whatever. She won't know who I'm talking about anyway."

Dixie was already reaching for her phone.

"And tell her you're staying at Lia's tonight or something," I added.

This made her pause. It was a little more insurance, I told myself, keeping her with me, knowing whether or not she was talking to Mom or Dad and what she was telling them.

"What am I doing tonight?" Dixie asked.

The bus got deeper into downtown, the touristy part, the convention center and the piers. If I'd been alone, I would have kept getting on buses all day and all night, until I was in another state. But I couldn't take Dixie that far away from home, not if she didn't want to go.

"I'm not sure," I said, honest. "We'll get off at the next stop for now."

Dixie tapped her fingers on the side of her phone, then typed out a message and sent it. "Okay. I told her."

We landed on the pavement of a busy street, everyone moving with purpose and confidence. I spun in a slow circle on the corner while Dixie waited for me to tell us what we were doing. "Come on," I said, and led her down toward the water. We could sit and watch the boats and ferries and gulls.

"I'm starving," Dixie said.

"There's food down there."

I found her a coffee shop where she could get a toasted, buttered poppy seed bagel the way she liked. I used to make that for her for an after-school snack, and for lunch in the summers when we were at home together while Mom worked.

We walked a little, then sat on a bench near the ferry dock. "Did Mom reply?" I asked.

Dixie shook her head and unwrapped enough of her bagel that she could take a bite.

A ferry, slow and huge, like a floating office building, was coming in from one of the islands. "Remember when we used to play runaway?"

She chewed, her eyes fixed on the water. "Yeah, I remember," she said. "Not like I'd forget."

"Pretend this is like that. Only we're not trapped in the apartment. We can do anything we want." I knew how naive it sounded, how naive it *was*, but I needed a little more time to work out exactly what I was doing. Also, the ten-year-old in me really wanted it to be like that, even for a little while.

Dixie's phone went off. She passed it to me after reading.

just woke up. that shit knocked me out

"At least she's not pretending she was 'tired' or something," I said.

"It's not such a big deal. Everybody takes pills."

"No they don't."

I was holding the phone when Mom's next message buzzed through.

my back is still killing me and I wonder if you can get me a little more? maybe drop it by before you go to lia's

I handed Dixie the phone and watched the ferry move into its berth. Mom and Dad were both making this easy for me. Dixie put her bagel down on the bench and stood. "I'm calling her."

"Dixie—"

"I'm not going to tell her anything." In a second she was talking to Mom. "You should probably just try to get to the doctor, Mom," she said. "No one has anything."

Pause.

"I know. But there's—"

She glanced at me and moved a few feet away.

"It's not that easy!"

She hugged herself with one arm and stared at the ground, listening.

"I'm sorry— Yes, I am! . . . Then go to the doctor. . . . Did you even ask? . . . Sorry. I'll try. Sorry."

She didn't come back to the bench. Instead she moved closer to the water and leaned on the railing there. I picked up what was left of her bagel and went to her. "Here."

"You can have it."

I tore off a chunk and threw it at a cluster of gulls in the water. They flapped and dived, then looked to me for more. I threw piece after piece at them until it was gone.

"I want to go home," Dixie said suddenly.

"Why? No."

"Yeah, this is dumb."

"You shouldn't have called," I said. "She makes *you* feel guilty for stuff *she* does."

She shoved her hands in her jacket pockets and crossed the street, away from me, back toward where we'd come from. I followed, walking fast, my backpack bouncing a little on my shoulders.

"Can't you see how messed up that is?" I asked.

"She just needs . . ." Dixie couldn't finish the sentence. Then she walked on as if she was trying to get away from me.

We were on a steep hill now with our backs to the water. I let myself fall farther behind. *Maybe I should let her go,* I thought. *Everything would be easier without her anyway.* If we were going to abandon each other, this was as good a time as any.

The practical part of me argued no, this was *not* as good a time as any, because now I wouldn't have my head start if she chose to tell Dad or Mom. But it wasn't only that making me chase after her.

"Dixie!"

She slowed.

At least *I* could see what was so wrong with our family. Dixie didn't have that yet. Glimpses, but not the whole picture. Maybe that was one last thing I could give her, one last way I could take care of her. Playing the runaway game one more time.

"One night," I said when I'd caught up to her.

She finally turned. We were both breathing heavily from the climb. I found myself smiling.

"Let's have this one night," I said. "We'll go to a fancy hotel. We'll order room service. You're right. My idea about leaving is dumb. I'm . . . I'm probably overreacting like I always do, but let's have a night and tomorrow we can go home and put the money back exactly like it was. Let's at least get something out of it." I don't like that I manipulated her that way. Maybe that made me no better than Dad. "And Dad will come whenever, and if he figures out there's a little missing, what can he say?"

She folded her arms. "He'll be pissed."

"We just keep pretending we don't know anything about it. Anyway, so what. Come on, Dixie."

I told myself I was doing it for her, even while thinking: *Choose me. Choose me over them. Let's go to the forest, let's go to space.*

"He owes it to us," I said, knowing I almost had her. "They both do."

She glanced down the street toward where we would get a bus if we were going home. "I just want things to be like they were."

"Like they were when?" I asked.

"You know, when Dad was going to have a club and we would dance around the apartment, all four of us, and . . ." She shrugged "I don't know. Like it was."

I knew what she meant and I understood how she'd come to believe it. We lied to ourselves as much as anyone lied to us. You have to, when you're a kid, if you want to get through it.

I held Dixie's wrist and expected her to jerk it away. But she kept still.

"Dixie," I said. "It was never like that."

When I told Dixie "never," I really meant never.

The second part of the family history I wrote for Mr. Bergstrom was about our grandparents. Or grandmothers,

I guess. Before I read it to him, I said, "This is the end because this is all I know, and I only know what my mom and dad and uncle talked about, or what they told me, or what I heard my mom tell her friend Roxanne."

"Looks like you have a lot to say," he said, noticing again how many pages I had.

"I don't know if it says anything," I told him. "Or if it's even true. It's just what I know."

Grandma Alice, my mom's mom, raised her and my uncle Ivan mostly by herself. She worked as a bank teller and they had a little house in a suburb of Portland. Mom and Ivan ate frozen dinners in front of the TV, and Grandma Alice gave them each a list of chores to do so that she didn't have to spend all her time after work cooking and cleaning. When she came home, she'd make a drink and put her feet up and smoke cigarettes while they all watched TV, and she'd make another drink and another, then go to sleep. On Friday and Saturday nights she went on dates. On Sunday mornings, sometimes she took Mom and Ivan to the Greek Orthodox church and sometimes she let them do whatever they wanted as long as they didn't bother her while she slept. Sunday afternoons she'd phone her own mother and make the kids talk to her, and then take the phone back and end up talking loud in Greek and crying, and Sunday nights after these conversations she'd go to her room and stay there until Monday morning, when they'd do the whole week over again.

I don't think any of that stuff made her a bad mother or person. Not food from a microwave or going on dates or anything. She provided for her kids way better than my parents ever provided for me, and she never walked out on them. But she still left them. Because of how she went to her room or drank when she was sad, how she carried pain all by herself and didn't show them how sometimes other people could help. How she fought with her mother in Greek and never told Mom or Ivan what they fought about or what made her cry. That's the same as being left, in some ways, or it feels like it. I know.

Grandma Alice hated my father from the first time my mom brought him home. She saw the grunge clothes and long hair and told my mom she'd wind up getting left, like her. Mom married Dad anyway and Grandma Alice still hated him; three years later, when I was two, she found out she had pancreatic cancer, and four months after that she died.

So that's my mom's mom.

My dad's mom, Grandma Jacobs, never had a career or anything. She depended on the men that came and went—including my dad's dad—to give her enough money to get by. She fought and scratched for it. "Fought and scratched" was how my dad put it when he talked about her to me and Dixie. Sometimes he'd say it with pride, like she was his hero, and sometimes he'd say it like he hated her.

The other thing I know is that she cooked. She got up every day and made breakfast for my dad. He was an only child. She packed him lunches for school and made his dinners.

Grandma Alice didn't tell Mom and Ivan anything, but Grandma Jacobs told my dad everything. I don't know which is worse, because when she didn't have a man around to take care of her, my dad was supposed to do it and she told him so. "You're all I've got, Rusty. Me and you." She wrote up lists of careers my dad could go into that paid a lot. That way he could take care of her. Pilot. Dentist. Investment banker.

"How about rock star?" he'd say. "Don't forget to put rock star on the list."

He said she told him he didn't have that kind of talent, or that kind of luck. She got older and had fewer boyfriends, and the ones she did have were mostly married. For my dad, being the man of the house meant he stayed home with his mom when he was in high school even if he wanted to be with his friends. Being the man of the house meant breaking his date for his junior prom because his mom was getting over being dumped by a guy and needed him home with her. It meant coming up with money somehow when they were short and bills couldn't wait.

When Grandma Jacobs got mad at people, she cut them off. That's what she did with her parents. She used to give my dad the silent treatment if he did something that made her unhappy. Usually what made her unhappy was my dad not giving her enough attention, or him caring about anyone other than her. She must have thought there wasn't enough love, to take or to give, like there was always a shortage one way or another.

When my dad met my mom, Grandma Jacobs thought all the love that belonged to her was going away, and she gave him the permanent silent treatment. To her, my mom was just the person who took away her son and then ruined his life by encouraging his rock star dreams. After they got married, Grandma Jacobs never talked to my dad again. I don't even think she knows Dixie or I exist.

I guess both my parents learned from theirs that men leave, and women stay around but don't really want to. They wanted to be different, but there was no one to show them how.

13.

DIXIE AND I walked the avenues. At each corner, I looked down toward the water. You'd think someone who spent her whole life in Seattle would get sick of seeing water, but we couldn't see it from our apartment, our neighborhood. I always knew it was there but it was for other people: tourists, professionals, people with money.

We were people with money now and we could claim it, too—the view, the blue-green expanse of the Sound, the slice of crystal-clear sky between the water and the layer of quilted clouds.

Dixie got slower and slower until I realized I was

walking alone. I turned around. She was on the phone. I went back to her.

" . . . so I told her I'm staying with you tonight, okay?" Lia.

"Thanks. Not like she's going to ask, but."

She listened, and glanced at me.

"Me and my sister have to take care of something. We won't be at school tomorrow, but don't worry. Just say we're sick if anyone asks."

Then she spent a long time mostly listening and came to a total stop, leaning against a building. Laughing, saying "I know" and "What?" and "Oh my god."

I hadn't had a best friend since seventh grade, when I'd go to Miriam Reed's house all the time. Our favorite thing was closing her bedroom door and putting on music and dancing around, singing into our fists like they were microphones, and buying enough candy for ten people and eating it all. Then, in the summer between seventh grade and eighth grade, she stopped inviting me over and made a whole new group of friends, and I'd still see her at school all the time but it was like our whole history had been erased.

"I'll call you tomorrow," Dixie was saying. She put her phone back in her pocket.

"Don't tell her about the money," I said.

"No shit."

We started walking again. We passed three hotels before Dixie asked, "What's our plan?"

"I'm just checking them all out." Which wasn't true. Every time we came near one, I thought, *This is the one*, but then I had no idea what to do next. "It has to be the right place."

"Okay. When we find the right place, what's our *plan*?"

"Go in and get a room?"

"You can't just walk in and get a room."

I stopped. "Why not?"

She sighed. "It's a hotel, Gem. Have you ever been in a hotel?"

Of course I'd never been in a hotel, she knew that. "Have *you*?"

She dug around in her bag and handed me a driver's license with her picture on it. Only it said her name was Amy King and that she was nineteen and lived in Shoreline.

"Where'd you get this?"

"Me and Lia both have them. We wanted to get into eighteen-and-over clubs. Like Mom and Dad used to do when they were our age. Come on." She started walking back in the direction we'd come from. "It has to be somewhere not too businessy. And not *too* nice but still nice enough. Hang on." She stepped to the edge of the sidewalk and crouched over her schoolbag. She pulled out a hair-brush and handed it to me, then a scarf that she twisted around her neck to cover the skin her V-neck left exposed. "We don't want them thinking we're, like, teen prostitutes or something. There are a lot of them down here."

I brushed my hair, but there wasn't much else I could do other than wipe bagel crumbs off my sweater. We started walking again, and I let myself fall behind, suddenly feeling uncertain and incapable. I watched her walk with the confidence she always had at school. I don't know if she'd copied it from other people, or if she created it out of thin air by sheer force of will. All I knew was she didn't get it from me.

She talked over her shoulder. "Let's go back to that one we passed a couple of blocks ago. With the fountain in the lobby."

I hadn't noticed it.

"Let me do the talking," she added.

Dixie led us into the place she deemed most likely to take our cash. The thing that she'd thought was a fountain in the lobby turned out to be a big stone sculpture, no water. We walked around it and then Dixie stepped right up to the counter. I lurked behind her, ready to pull a bundle of fifties from my bag.

The woman working the desk wore a neat blue suit and had shiny black hair pulled into a tight bun and one perfect curl gelled just in front of her ear. "How can I help you?"

"Do you have any rooms available? We don't have a reservation."

"How many nights?"

"Just tonight."

Her eyes flicked from Dixie to me, and back to Dixie.

"We missed our ferry," Dixie explained. "All we have is cash, okay?"

"It's early. The ferries run all day, and late at night."

"Well, we missed the one we were *supposed* to get and now no one can pick us up on the other side until tomorrow."

"We don't normally . . ." The woman glanced behind her. "You'd have to put an extra three hundred down as a deposit, is the thing." She said it like she was certain we wouldn't have that much.

"Okay," Dixie said.

The woman lifted her dark eyebrows. "And I need to see ID."

Dixie slid her license across the shiny black marble. "How much total?"

She looked at the license, looked at Dixie. I don't know if she believed Dixie was nineteen, but I'd already stepped forward to start counting cash onto the marble. She clicked some things on her computer. "With the deposit and the cash-rate room . . . Two queens all right?"

"Yes."

"And taxes and fees . . ." She watched me. "Five ninety-seven."

I stopped counting. It was so much. Dixie nodded her head at me. "Put extra," she said quietly. "For room service and everything. Anyway, we get the deposit back."

"*If* the room is in good condition at checkout," the woman said. "No smoking anywhere in the room. That includes the bathroom. And checkout takes a little extra time. You'll need to plan for that."

The woman handed a piece of paper over for Dixie to fill in and sign. I watched her write *Amy King* and the address from the ID. I counted out the money and the woman whisked it away with another glance over her shoulder, and in a minute we had two key cards.

"Thank you, Ms. King. Enjoy your stay."

Dixie's eyes narrowed in a certain way and I knew something had happened that I hadn't noticed. "I need a receipt. For the deposit."

"I'm sorry?" The woman stared at us.

"I need a *receipt*," Dixie said again, her voice raised.

I sensed someone behind me and thought, *This is it—we're caught.* But when I turned, it was only a couple with suitcases, waiting to check in next. Dixie turned around to them and said, "I'm just waiting for my receipt because she took our cash."

The woman behind the counter smiled tightly. "I'm sorry. Of course."

Dixie double-checked everything on the receipt before we headed to the elevator. Once we were inside and zooming up to the eleventh floor, she said, "That bitch was going to try to keep our deposit."

It hadn't even crossed my mind that could happen. What other kinds of stuff didn't I know? "Where did you get that ID?" I asked her again.

"Nowhere. I got it. I mean, you have to ask around and then you get a name or an address and you go do it." She shrugged, as if it was just that easy.

The doors swished open and we found our room. Dixie used her key card, and before I could see what was inside, she turned to me with a smile and said, "Okay, this was actually a really good idea."

14.

THE ROOM had striped wallpaper, cream and gold. I'd never seen anything like that. Each bed seemed twice as big as our beds at home, and each was covered with pillows. There were an armchair and footrest by the window, a fancy wooden desk, a huge TV on top of a dresser, bedside tables with glass lamps, and a beige-and-brown flowered carpet.

"I'm taking this one," Dixie said, throwing her bag and jacket on the bed closest to the window. She pulled back the gauzy curtains. "Check out the view."

I went over to her. From as high as we were, we could see the whole waterfront, from the Ferris wheel turning over Elliott Bay to the green of the parkway on the other end and all the way across to the islands. I didn't know which island was which, or the names of all the things I was seeing. I knew about as much as a tourist.

Dixie tapped my foot with hers. "Say something."

I wanted to be happy, like her. Excited. Instead, looking at the incredible view left me hollowed out. All I could see was what wasn't there. I touched the window. "We've lived here our whole lives and Mom and Dad never took us to the Ferris wheel. Or the market. Or any of this stuff."

I felt her eyes on me. Then she said, "Dad took me on the Ferris wheel once. It's not that great, trust me."

Something pinged around in the hollow inside me, bouncing painfully between my stomach and heart. "When?"

"I don't know. Whenever. I was little. Probably when you were in school but I hadn't started yet."

I stared at her and knew from her face that mine showed everything I felt.

Dixie flopped onto her bed. "Please, don't go all negative and sad right now, Gem. This was your idea. You're the one who wanted to have one great night, and now I want to enjoy it. If you spend the whole time moping, I'm going to be pissed." She swung her legs over the side of the bed and unlaced her boots. Dixie and Dad, on the Ferris wheel. He probably took her to the market, too, and who knows where else.

I turned my back on the window, on her, and went to the other bed. I slipped the backpack off my shoulders and took my jacket off, and I explored the rest of the room. There was a little nook where you could put your suitcase, I guess, if you were a normal traveler. I studied the emergency escape route information on the door. "Don't go in the elevator if there's a fire," I said over my shoulder.

"Alrighty." Dixie had turned on the TV and was flipping through channels with the volume low.

I opened the closet. There were extra blankets and pillows, an iron and ironing board, and two fluffy white robes. I put one on over my clothes. "Look."

"What."

"Look!"

Dixie turned her head to see me running my hands up and down the robe, smiling to prove I didn't really care about the Ferris wheel thing. I waited for her to roll her eyes, tell me I was being dumb. But she sat up. "I want one."

I got the other one out of the closet and came close enough to her to throw it.

"It's so soft." She spread it over her like a blanket.

With the sleeves of the robe hanging down to my knuckles, I went into the bathroom. It wasn't huge the way I thought a bathroom in a hotel like this should be, but it still impressed me. Everything was this white marble, swirled with a different kind of white that seemed to glow. White floor, white sink, white toilet, white tub and shower with a white-and-gold curtain.

"I'm taking a bath," I said.

Dixie's eyes were closed, but she'd left the TV on. "Mmmkay," she said drowsily.

I took off the robe, got out of my clothes, and put the robe back on. I folded my jeans and my sweater, my underwear and socks, into a neat pile that I put on the table closest to my bed.

Then I thought, *Maybe I should take the backpack into the bathroom.* It's not that I thought Dixie would take it, I just . . . I don't know, maybe I did think that. I wanted it with me. I laid it on the bathroom floor, then started running hot water in the tub. A basket on the sink held four rolled-up washcloths and little bottles of shampoo, conditioner, lotion, and shower gel. I opened the shower gel and smelled it. Lemons. I squeezed the whole bottle into the running water and adjusted the temperature. Soon the tub was all bubbles.

I locked the door, hung the robe on a hook on the back of it, and stepped into the water. I let the faucet run until my whole body disappeared under the lemon bubbles. When I closed my eyes, I saw Dixie and Dad on the Ferris wheel, the image of them burned onto my retinas as if

I'd just seen it in bright sun.

With everything that had happened, the last week, the last day, our whole lives, I don't know why that one little thing hurt so much.

I opened my eyes and let my legs float and my feet pop out of the water. My toenails were ragged and needed to be cut but my legs were still smooth from shaving with the new razor. It wasn't fair to be mad at Dixie about the fact that Dad had spent more time with her. She was a kid. If I was going to blame anyone for that, it should be him.

But he hadn't been around to be mad at. Dixie always was.

I scooted my hips so that I could submerge my whole head in the water, and I rubbed my scalp with my fingers, then came back up just enough to expose my nose and mouth. My blood pulsed in my ears, the rushing of some faraway tide. I stayed under, listening and trying to think.

I was mad at myself, too. In the early hours that morning, with Dixie sleeping and me forcing myself to stay awake, I'd worked out an idea that might not have been detailed but was clean. Then I'd thought I would just go to school for the first half of the day, so that Mr. Bergstrom wouldn't worry that something had happened when I left with Dad. Then I'd wanted to thank Luca. And then I wanted to see her, only see her. To make sure she was all right and hadn't noticed the money missing and hadn't talked to anyone about it. I should have known better.

When my fingertips got wrinkly, I flipped the drain lever on the tub and got out. Bubbles clung to me and quietly hissed when I smothered them with one of the white towels. I wrapped another towel around my hair and then sat on the white bath mat with my back against the door and emptied the contents of the backpack onto the floor. It was all the money and then *The Grapes of Wrath* and a bunch of packs of Haciendas. I hadn't bothered bringing any school stuff to school except my reading journal, which I'd turned in because I guess I wanted to leave Mrs. Cantrell with a good impression of me.

I separated the money by denomination and made stacks on the white shelf under the sink, next to the folded towels. At first it seemed like I kept finding more and more fives. I hadn't even tried to guess at how much money was in the bag but it had seemed like a lot. Now, I wasn't too sure. Then I found a bundle of hundreds. Another of fifties. A few bundles of twenties. Then some loose fifties and hundreds.

None of it looked too new, or fake. Dad must have used money from the bag to buy all our groceries. We'd used it to get into this hotel. No one had looked at it twice; it had to be as real as it felt and looked and smelled.

Piles of paper, that was it. Piles of paper that were as

close as my dad had come to taking care of me for a long time, and he didn't even know it

I counted it three times. I hung up my towel and put my robe back on, combed out my hair with my fingers, put lotion on my legs. The whole time, I kept my eyes on the neat row of bills and tried to comprehend the number I'd come up with: twenty-seven thousand dollars, not counting the ones and fives. How long could a person live on that? At least a year, I thought, maybe closer to two if you were like me and you were really careful.

Dixie's knock on the door startled me. "Hurry up, I have to pee."

"Just a sec." I crouched on the floor and started to load the money back into the pack.

She pounded on the door again.

I stood up, money still piled on the shelf. It was impossible to hide what I'd been doing, and that would only make her trust me less when what I wanted was for her to trust me more. I let her in.

"I'm counting it."

Her robe was around her shoulders like a cape, her clothes still on; the back of her hair was sticking up from her nap. She stared at me, and at the money I was halfway done putting away.

"We should at least know how much it is," I added.

"What difference does it make? We're taking it back

tomorrow. You promised."

I didn't technically *promise*. "Aren't you even curious?"

After a pause she said, "Yeah. Okay."

I stood up, holding two bundles of twenties. I had four thousand dollars right in my hand. "It's about twenty thousand dollars," I said. "Not counting the ones and fives."

"That's all?" she asked, disappointed.

For a second, I didn't breathe. I hadn't meant to lie. "What do you mean, 'that's all'? That's a lot. Anyway, there's like another couple thousand in fives, probably." I pulled the ends of my damp hair over my shoulder and twisted the ends. "You can recount it if you want," I said. "You probably should. Maybe I got it wrong."

"Let me pee first."

"Okay." I put the twenties back on the towel shelf, got my book and cigarettes, and left the backpack as if I didn't care. I made myself not look back.

The TV was still on; I flipped channels and turned the volume up. When I couldn't stand it anymore, I stood outside the bathroom door and asked, "Are you counting it?"

"Can you not talk to me while I'm going to the bathroom?"

The minutes dragged on. I started to worry she was taking some of the money herself, hiding it in her clothes or her robe somewhere. When the door swung open, I stepped back and saw that everything looked exactly like I'd left it. "I'm *starving*," she said. "Let's order food."

I stared at the money. "We probably shouldn't leave it out like that. I'll put the rest back in the bag. Okay?"

"Go ahead." She pushed past me, and I loaded the money back in the bag and brought it out into the room. I slipped the bag into the space between my bed and my nightstand. Dixie sat on the edge of her bed flipping through a binder full of room service menus. "What do you want?"

"What is there?"

"Everything." She read aloud: "'All-American Cheeseburger Served with House-Made Pickled Onions,' 'Wood-Fired Pizzas with Seasonal Toppings.' 'Bacon-Truffle Macaroni and Local Cheese.' Everything. Fries, salads, pasta, steak, chicken. I'm getting salmon. And also the mac and cheese. And a hot fudge sundae." She held out the binder to me. "Don't take forever to decide."

I took it and picked a cheeseburger and fries, and a pizza with potatoes and goat cheese on it because I'd never heard of potatoes on pizza before and never had goat cheese. Also a dessert sampler. Dixie called it in, sounding like she ordered room service every day.

"I need to get a fake ID like yours," I said after she'd hung up.

"It comes in handy." She flipped the channels. "Let's watch a movie."

I retied my robe—it was almost big enough to wrap around me twice—and laid on my bed, shifting my dozen pillows around until I got comfortable. "When did you ever stay in a hotel before?" I asked.

She scrolled through the on-screen guide. "It was just one time."

"When? With who?"

She dropped the hand holding the remote to her side. "I hate it when you do that."

"What?"

"Interrogate me."

"I'm just asking questions."

"Well, you ask them like . . . I don't know. Like I have to answer to you. I mean, I can have secrets. Everybody does."

"Maybe they shouldn't," I said. "Look what having secrets does to Mom and Dad."

"You have them, too, Gem." She lifted the remote and scrolled through a few more screens. "Romantic comedy or action?"

"I don't care," I said. "Romantic comedy, I guess." She ordered a movie off the screen. "What was it like?" I asked. "The Ferris wheel."

She sighed. I thought about my own secrets, and how

they made me feel protected. Like not telling Mr. Berg-strom every single thing. Like having my cigarettes. And like I knew I would have kept the money secret if I'd been alone when I found it. Maybe Dixie's secrets made her feel protected, too.

"What was it like?" I asked again. "Were you scared?"

"I *told* you. It was nothing. I didn't like it."

I pictured her and Dad, swinging at the top with a view of everything, Dixie cuddled up to him, him telling her not to be afraid.

"Has either of them texted again or anything?"

"I don't know. I turned my phone off because my char-ger is at home. I want to save the battery." She paused the movie, then said, "Will you please relax? I can tell you're all tense over there." Then, in a nicer tone, she added: "We're here, we're going to pig out on really good food, and then tomorrow we have to go back to dealing with all the usual shit. So just enjoy being here."

She sounded happy.

"No one knows where we are, Gem," she continued. "Doesn't that feel amazing?"

I would not be going to back the usual shit, I wanted to tell her. "Yeah," I said. "It does."

When the food came, we forgot about everything else. We'd never had anything like it. Every detail of my burger was perfect, from the way the cheese melted without turning into rubber to the little pieces of toasted onion that were part of the bun. The fries were crisp and salty and came with homemade ketchup.

"Why would anyone make their own ketchup?" Dixie asked.

"I don't know, but it's good." I made Dixie try it, and she made me try her mac and cheese. After tasting each other's food, we decided to move it all onto her bed so we could both eat everything.

"Mom would be impressed," Dixie said. "Us sharing."

I didn't want Mom with us in this moment. I said mm-hmm quickly and shifted my attention to the pizza before a clear picture of her could form in my mind. "Look how thin the potatoes are sliced." I peeled one off the pizza and held it up. We could see the glow of the TV right through it.

"I might be sick pretty soon." She'd eaten her hot fudge sundae first so the ice cream wouldn't melt, and had slowed down halfway through her salmon.

"Not me." I could eat and eat; my stomach felt bottomless for this. This wasn't rock-heavy meat loaf and side dishes from a box like Dad had fixed us. "I want to eat like this every day for the rest of my life," I said.

Dixie groaned and put down the forkful of food she'd been about to eat. "Maybe we can both get jobs that make us rich," she said. "We can fly around the world first class and eat potato pizzas in Italy."

She'd never talked about us as a "we" that would exist at some point in the future. I wondered if the thought came to her just because of this moment, or if it was something she thought about other times but didn't say.

The money we had wasn't enough for all that. Anyway, it didn't really matter to me, world travel and fancy food. All I wanted was to make ends meet without needing anyone else to help me. And I wanted that only because I wanted a home that felt like home should feel. Safe. A place you go where you know there won't be any bad surprises and you can be even more who you are, not less.

Dixie and I laughed together at the romantic comedy, the stupidity of it. We made fun of how the couple kissed, and we finally gave up and put the trays of what was left of our food out into the hall for the housekeeping people to pick up, like the lady who'd brought it up said to. The big window was rain streaked by the end of our movie. We watched the city lights glisten.

Right then, with the dream of fancy traveling together, and us getting along, full of food, and Dixie believing that soon things would go back to the way she was used to them being, we were as happy as we were going to get.

15.

WHEN I would think about people who could have helped us, either before things got bad or after they did—people who maybe should have helped us—the first one was Uncle Ivan. I never thought he wouldn't be in our lives. Not like he was the most reliable person in the world—he'd be around, then he'd disappear, like most adults I knew other than my teachers. But he always came back.

When we were younger, Mom would tell us stories from when they were kids, getting into trouble their mother never knew about while she was at work, and then later, running around Portland in their teens. She'd get mad at me and Dixie for fighting. "You guys should be each other's best friends. You're the only ones who know what it's like to be in your family. You'll see when you're older," she said. "In the end, you're all each other has. Like me and Ivan."

They talked on the phone all the time. Then not as much. Then, she didn't have him. He met a woman he loved and moved to Idaho and got married without even inviting us to the wedding. He came that one time to help my mom kick my dad out, and that was the last time we saw him. He has a baby now. My cousin. I don't know what happened with Uncle Ivan and my mom, but she didn't seem mad about it. There were a lot of times I thought about trying to find out his number and call him, but whenever I asked my mom if I could, she said, "You leave your uncle Ivan alone. He's got a good life now."

I didn't know what that meant except that us being in it would turn it from good to bad, and I didn't want to do that to him.

Then there was Roxanne, my mother's ex-best friend. They'd met at one of my mom's jobs a long time ago, and they talked every day. She'd come over to our apartment and Mom would tell her what was going on with my dad and his using or his girlfriends or his not having a job, and Roxanne would commiserate and they'd get high together. But also she would look at me and Dixie sometimes, and smile and play with us, and then tell my mom maybe there were certain things my mom shouldn't say with us sitting right there.

"They can hear you, Adri," Roxanne would say, nodding her head our way and flipping her black ponytail over her shoulder.

Every year, on the anniversary of Kurt Cobain's death, they got together to listen to *Nevermind*—the Nirvana album that came out when Mom and Roxanne were fifteen—and make drinks and light candles in his memory. Sometimes my dad was there. One time, my dad and Roxanne danced around to "Lithium" while my mom went to the freezer to get more ice. Dixie and I were jumping up and down next to them. Then, real fast, Dad moved his hand down Roxanne's hip and whispered something in her ear. When Mom emerged with the ice, Roxanne was pushing Dad away and saying, "Don't pull that shit with me, Russ. Especially in front of the girls. Dumbass."

She turned and danced with me, and Dad got his cigarettes and went out for a smoke.

"Last straw yet, Adri?" Roxanne asked Mom between songs.

Mom took Roxanne's hands and swayed with her to "Polly" and said, "Not tonight. Tonight is our night. Yours and mine and Kurt's."

Later, Roxanne and Mom got sober together. They'd

go to meetings and call each other when they wanted to drink or to use, and they'd celebrate every new sober month by ordering pizza and watching a favorite movie. Something with Julia Roberts, usually, or one of the Terminator movies. They'd toast with diet soda and eat chocolate until they got sick.

When I was in fifth grade, I got a cold and then strep throat, and Mom didn't take me to the doctor soon enough and the strep went into my kidneys. My lower back hurt so bad. I stayed with Roxanne a few days, because it was one of Dad's gone times and Mom couldn't get off work to take care of me when I'd normally be at school. Roxanne made me a warm bath every day with bath salts that smelled like eucalyptus and lavender, and I'd sit in it until the water stopped being warm enough, and she'd stay with me in the bathroom, reading a book or a magazine out loud to take my mind off how much my back ached. I remember her reading me a magazine story about how to grow out your bangs.

I didn't want to go home that time and felt guilty for wishing I didn't have to. I never thought there would be a time when Roxanne wasn't there, same as with Uncle Ivan.

Around the time Dad left for good, Mom started drinking again. Then doing more. And she wasn't going to the meetings or spending very much time at all with

Roxanne. They still talked on the phone a lot, but it was mostly fighting. I'd listen to Mom's side of the conversation and hear stuff like:

I don't need that. I'm fine.

Only wine and pot! Nothing hard, I swear.

Don't judge me, Rox. . . . What do you call it, then?

I can't deal with that higher power shit. I never could. You know that.

Gradually we stopped hearing about her. I don't think Mom ever got over it. She had other friends afterward but none that she loved like she loved Roxanne. Love like the love she had for us—the biggest and strongest love she could feel, still easily blown over by her selfishness or addiction or whatever it was that kept her from being able to be . . . I don't know . . . different.

All her real friends cleaned up and disappeared, and she replaced them with disposable friends who were mostly there to listen to her complain about Dad, other men, or work, or to party with her. I wanted Mom to be like Roxanne. Or Roxanne to be our mom. She was evidence that a person could change. I think she wanted to help, and maybe she tried. But Mom was our link to her and that link got broken, and there was nothing we could do about that.

Stuff happens to most people. One thing going wrong, I mean. One family member missing a chance to help.

One who cuts you off. One person with her own shit to deal with.

One of those things isn't enough to send you falling through the cracks.

But all of them together, they accumulate. An abandoned mother here. A missing uncle there. A disappearing father two generations back. A friendship broken by fear or mistrust or addiction. Genes that make you vulnerable to certain problems. Two children who weren't loved right meeting up when they're not really adults yet and having two more children who aren't loved right.

It adds up. It all adds up.

16.

THE CLOCK on the bedside table said 3:17 when I woke with an ache that proved me wrong in thinking my stomach could handle anything. I got up to use the bathroom; then I couldn't fall back to sleep. Dixie was curled in a ball facing me.

"Dixie?" I whispered. She didn't move.

Quietly, I slipped into the bathroom again, taking the backpack with me.

Only seven thousand, I told myself, counting out a combination of hundreds and fifties and twenties. It wasn't a lot. A small safety net. I wrapped that amount in a hotel washcloth, then splashed water on my face. I got a glass off the sink and filled it to take back to bed with me. I put the washcloth under my pillow and then returned the backpack to where it had been.

Lying down only made my aching stomach feel heavier, so I sat in the armchair by the window and looked out over the lights and the water, sipping from my glass.

I sat there long enough to watch the slow brightening of dawn, a reverse fade from black to dark blue to purple and deep gray. It was pretty, but I wanted it to stop. With it came reality, an end to room service and movies and bubble baths and not having to think about what would come next.

Dixie made a waking-up noise, something between a sigh and a groan. I turned to see her rolling over toward the window, her eyes open. "Why are you awake?" she whimpered.

"My stomach. I needed to sit up."

She gathered a pillow against her body and spooned it. "S'pretty," she said, half into the pillow.

"I wish we lived near the water."

"We do."

"I mean, I wish we lived where we could *see* the water." Life would feel more open, I imagined. You'd never have to feel trapped, with all of that water and sky.

We watched the sky fade into lighter and lighter gray. A ferry made its way out onto the Sound.

"Maybe we could move," Dixie said. "I mean, like maybe me and you and Mom could find a new place, a better place. . . ." She shifted her blankets and pillows around and closed her eyes, dreamy. "She needs to get a job she can do during the day. Like in an office. Something that pays more, where she could come home at normal times."

I watched her face, how young and I guess innocent it looked. She might be carrying around some piece of plastic saying she was nineteen. She might know how to check into a hotel and keep us from getting ripped off. She might have boyfriends and go to clubs and never have to eat lunch alone. But there was so much she still hadn't learned—or at least stuff she hadn't let herself know. That's what I mean by innocent, thinking Mom could— would—get a good-paying, normal-hours job.

I could have asked: *Why are we here, Dixie? Remember what Mom was doing when we last saw her?* That was part of my purpose, wasn't it, to give her the eyes to see the truth? But maybe it was okay to be innocent like that, maybe it was good. Just because I couldn't be like that didn't make it a bad way to be.

"Do you want to call down for coffee or something?" I asked her.

She scooted over on the bed so she could reach the room phone, dragging her blankets with her. After she ordered coffee and hot chocolate and some food, I said we should check her phone.

"I don't want to hear them," she said. "I don't want to know."

"We have to know. Then we can decide what to do."

She propped herself up with a pillow. "What we do is hang around until checkout, go home, put the money back and pretend we don't know anything about it. Like we said."

"Dixie . . ." I started.

"What?"

It wasn't the right time. If she got mad at me now, she could still call Dad, ruin things for me. "Don't you want to know how much trouble we're going to be in? To prepare?"

"Fine." She got her phone off the bedside table and turned it on.

We waited what seemed like forever for it to come on and find a signal. Then it buzzed. Dixie showed me the screen. There was a text from Dad.

mom says you're at some sleepover. call when you get this

"He went back to the apartment?" I said. Or maybe called her. Either way, Mom was clear enough to talk to him and tell him where we supposedly were. But maybe he hadn't been there, physically, to check under the bed. . . .

"There's a voice mail from him, too," Dixie said.

"Put it on speaker."

She pushed the blanket off her shoulders. "Why? I don't even want to hear it."

I ran my fingers over the fabric of the armchair. I could have been so far away by now. Instead I was maybe three miles from home, because I didn't leave her.

"I mean, what difference does it make?" she asked. "It's over, Gem. We have to go home."

I looked at the phone in her hands as if Dad could reach through it and take everything away from me. "Can he track us with that?"

She looked at me; I couldn't read her expression. Afraid of Dad, or frustrated with me, or only tired. "I don't know."

A loud knock in the door made us both jump. Then a woman's voice on the other side of it said, "Room service."

Dixie held down the power button to turn the phone off, and I got up. I checked through the peephole that it really was room service, then stood back while the woman, not much older than us, wheeled in a little cart. She turned the cart into a table and uncovered a basket of croissants and rolls and pastries next to our pot of coffee and mugs of hot chocolate.

"Can I get you anything else?" she asked, standing with her hands folded in front of her.

I shook my head and signed *Amy King* to the bill, and then she left.

We were subdued, not giddy over the food like we'd been the night before. Me, because of worrying I'd messed up my best chance to leave. Dixie, probably because she knew it was unlikely now that she could avoid trouble with Dad. We decided to move the table over to the window. We sat down with our view of the water, the islands, the ferries coming and going, me in the armchair and Dixie in the desk chair.

"I can't eat," she said, staring down at the white table-cloth.

But after a second she took a Danish out of the basket and nibbled at it. I poured her some coffee, then she poured that into her hot chocolate. She added sugar and kept her eyes on the window while she chewed and sipped. Maybe it was that she needed to think, but it felt like the silent treatment.

"Are you mad at me?" I asked.

"What am I going to say?" she asked. "When I call him? I have to tell him we spent some of it."

I tore into a croissant; it collapsed and shed flakes all over my plate, the table, the front of my robe. *I,* she said. To Dad, I guess, it *was* all about her—after all, he hadn't mentioned me in his text. I could be *I,* too. *I'd* found the money. *I* didn't have to show it to her.

"You don't have to call," I said.

"Yes I do." Then she said, "You should have left it there like you said you would that night. This is so dumb."

This is so dumb, Gem. You are *so dumb, Gem.*

I did show it to her, though. And since then I'd been thinking of us more and more as a "we," whether or not I wanted to, whether or not I should.

"We" was a trap. I could almost feel it on me like a straitjacket.

What's the box? Mr. Bergstrom had asked when I drew it around the whiteboard version of me.

What I should have drawn was a cage.

The cage was Mom. The cage was Dad. The cage was our apartment, the empty fridge, the trips to the dark laundry room. The cage was Dixie—pushing her in her stroller and walking her to school and feeding her and dressing her and keeping her busy when she was scared, entertained when she was bored. The cage was me being responsible for all of it, all of them, being the responsible one in the family as far back as I could remember. It was guilt, it was being misunderstood and feeling accused.

Dixie stared at me, waiting for a reply.

I hadn't lost it in months and I wouldn't do it in front of her. I breathed. My fingers itched for a Hacienda. The pebble-tears built up inside my throat. This time I wasn't going to let myself be responsible.

"He's the one who put it there," I managed.

"I know, but—"

"He's the one who put it there." I let my fist pound on my leg. Just once, enough to hurt. A tiny release. "*He's* the one. *He's* the one."

She set her Danish down. "Okay. Don't get like—"

"*He's* the one. And Mom." I crossed my arms over my body and held on to bunches of my robe, pulling at them as hard as I could. "Him and Mom, and our whole lives they didn't take *care* of us."

"Gem," she said slowly, "do not go apeshit right now. Please."

"I'm not going back home."

"You—"

"I mean it, Dixie. I'm not going back." The more I said it, the more the straitjacket loosened.

"What are you going to do? You can't just . . . not go back."

"Yes I can." It would actually be easy. Simple, anyway. As simple as never setting foot in that building again. My breathing got deeper.

I could be responsible for me, no one else.

"You're not taking the money, Gem," she said, almost with a laugh. "If that's what you're thinking."

"I already took it."

"I can't go home without it, Gem. He'll never believe I don't know where it is." She shook her head. "You didn't even know how to get into a hotel. You're gonna, like, strike out on your own now?"

I stood up. I imagined throwing myself onto the bed and smashing my face into a pillow and screaming until all of the pebbles were out of my throat. What would she think of me then? Would it make her understand me, or understand anything? Would it only prove she was right, that it was stupid to think I could go out into the world on my own?

Maybe she *was* right.

Don't think that, Gem. Don't betray yourself now.

"Okay," I said. "If you really want to give it back to him, if that's what you want to do, go ahead." I pointed to where I'd stashed the backpack, knowing I still had my seven thousand dollars under my pillow. "If you feel guilty about taking something from him after a whole life of him taking from us, if you think giving this money back is going to . . . I don't know, make him love you or something, if you think it's going to solve all the problems and he's going to come around and be a great father and have an explanation that makes total sense for why he's stashing drug money or whatever it is in our room the day after coming back out of the blue with hardly any warning or reason, then good. Good for you. Maybe you're right. Maybe he has an honest reason. Maybe he's a great father. Turn the phone back on. Listen to the voice mail. He probably called to come clean about the money and say how much he loves you and that he understands why you might be upset about him leaving it there. That's probably what he said."

Her face had slowly closed while I talked. Her eyes had filled; then the tears dried up. Her mouth didn't tremble like it did when she was going to cry. She was steady as a rock.

I let my robe drop to the floor and stood there naked. "I'm going to take a shower. Call him if you want. I don't care. As long as you know that he's using you."

Then her mouth did give way, a little bit.

"*He uses you,*" I said. "Not me. Because, of the two of us, you're the one who falls for it. You're the one who mistakes it for love."

Under the shower, I began to shake. I covered my face with a washcloth and let the scream tear through me until it was gone.

When I came out of the bathroom—wrapped in towels, my throat raw—Dixie was on her bed, holding her phone. "Fine."

"Fine what?" I asked.

"Fine whatever. I won't call him."

I just stared at her, and she put her phone on speaker and played me his voice mail:

"Hey where the hell are you? I, um— Look, I put something in your room just for safekeeping, okay, and I think you have it and it's really . . . Dixie, you need to answer your fucking phone and tell me where you are, and do not TELL anyone what you found, that would be very bad. I'm going to try to find you at school today. If I don't see you there, you'd better meet me back at the apartment later. And . . . listen, don't be a little shit about this. Show me I can trust you. Call me."

I sat on my bed and took off the towel I had around my hair. "You can take it if you want. Go to school. See him. I mean, if you want it to be over." And when he discovered there was seven thousand missing, she could blame it on me, and be right.

"I'm not . . . I'm not ready to do anything yet. I'm not saying I'm not going back. But what's the rush?"

I felt both relief and worry.

"And it's not my fault, Gem," she continued. "Maybe you're right. Maybe he doesn't really love me." She turned her phone back off. "But it's not my fault that he doesn't love you, either."

It didn't hurt. It didn't hurt to hear. I mean, I felt the pain of it but it was okay. It wasn't anything I hadn't already told myself a hundred times, that he hadn't demonstrated clearly enough. It was a fact like any other fact and it didn't kill me. I didn't turn into a pile of ash or disappear. I was still there. And so was Dixie.

17.

WE WOULD get on a ferry, we decided, like she'd told the front desk lady we were going to do. We would ride out to one of the islands. It didn't solve anything, and I had no plan beyond that. I couldn't and didn't want to force her to go back before she was ready. So we were stuck in not leaving, not going back, and not parting ways. Only filling time.

"I have to get a charger before we leave downtown," she said. "For my phone."

"Maybe we should just let it die."

"I have to have a phone, Gem. What if there's an emergency? What if we get lost? What if we get into trouble?"

Like this whole thing wasn't trouble and an emergency? "I get along without a phone."

"Aren't you a special snowflake." It was a typical Dixie comment, but without the typical venom.

Getting a charger meant staying put until after nine, when stores would be open. We figured if Dad did what he said he was going to do—show up at school, check at the apartment again—we had the morning before he'd even begin to realize we weren't at friends' houses, or even think about where else we might be. Or, not *we*. I had to remind myself that, from his messages, it seemed he had no idea I was involved, let alone that I was the one behind it. I wonder if he even thought of me at all.

Dixie showered. While she was in there, I took the washcloth with the money inside it out from under my pillow, put it deep into the pocket of my jacket.

When she came out in her robe and picked her shirt and jeans up off her bed, she said, "As long as we're going shopping, we might as well buy some clothes."

"I thought you were worried about Dad being angry about us spending money."

She shrugged. "Nothing expensive. Some extra underwear, T-shirts. I don't want to walk around in dirty clothes."

We got packed and agreed that we'd only spend as much as we got when we checked out of the hotel, whatever was left of the cash deposit. The rest of it, we'd leave untouched.

Dixie stood by the door with her jacket on and her schoolbag over her shoulder. She'd put on the scarf again and pinned her hair close to her head, and somehow done her makeup. I guess she always carried makeup to school with her.

"What?" she asked after I'd stared too long.

"Nothing," I said. "You look good. How do you always look good?"

"I don't."

"You do. I see you every day. I know."

She got that defiant expression I was so used to; then it went away and she said, "Thanks."

I went to the hotel window one last time, looking out at the puzzle of land and water, wondering where exactly I was headed.

Dixie presented our receipt at the front desk. We waited for them to make sure we hadn't trashed the room and to total up our room service expenses. Then we got our cash back.

"Thanks for doing all that," I told Dixie "Making sure we didn't get ripped off."

We were on the street, the sidewalks damp but some sun breaking through the low-lying clouds. After a night in a room with windows that didn't open, the air felt good. Dixie pointed us uphill, where the desk clerk had told her there was a place that would probably have the phone charger she needed.

"The time I was in a hotel before," she said as we walked, "it was me and Lia. We wanted to try out our fake IDs after we got them and we had some money from Lia's birthday. We'd seen it on TV a lot, people in hotels."

I kept quiet so she'd keep talking.

"This guy at the place we went—first he kind of accused us of being whores, then when we tried to get the deposit back in the morning, there was no record of it. Like, he'd just taken it. But it was our word against his, and me and Lia looked like . . . well, like me and Lia look. That's how I knew how hard it is if you don't have a credit card. And how shady some of these hotel people are."

"You spent the night at the hotel?" I asked, trying to keep up.

"Yeah. I told Mom I was sleeping over at Lia's house. Lia told her mom she was sleeping at mine." She shrugged. "We do that all the time."

We got to a corner; Dixie turned us left. There were plenty of those nights I'd been alone in our room when Dixie was at Lia's, or so I thought. "Why?" I asked. "What do you do?"

We kept walking, and from her silence I thought she

must be annoyed with my questions, me being the older one with no idea why someone our age might want to stay out all night, or lie about where she was. She was probably thinking how naive and embarrassing I was.

Then she stopped at the next corner to wait for the light to change, and she said, "We do stupid stuff, Gem. Just dumb stuff we shouldn't do. I wish . . ." The light changed and she turned to me with this look on her face that I read as a kind of being lost, or maybe an apology. "I guess this is just another dumb thing I'm doing."

"It's not dumb," I said.

"We'll see."

She never said what she wished.

We found the phone store, and when Dixie paid for the charger, she also asked the girl at the counter some other stuff about her phone.

"Could someone who had my number, like, track me?"

"Let me see your phone." The girl examined it and said, "Yeah, probably. I mean, it's not easy but it's possible. If you're really worried about someone finding you, just get a burner."

"A what?"

"A burner. Cheap, with prepaid minutes. New number."

"Like the one I had when I worked at the gift shop," I said to Dixie.

The girl leaned on the counter, tapping her blue-painted nails on the glass. "That's what I did when this guy I used to date was stalking me. I tossed my old phone, went through a few burners. I'd only give the numbers to people I trusted. If he found the number out, I threw the phone away and got a new one. Or I'd keep the phone but get a new SIM. Outsmarted that dickhead until he got tired of trying. They're right over there," she said, pointing to a rack along the wall.

"They're untraceable?" I asked.

"If you pay with cash. Basically." She studied us. "I mean, I assume the government isn't after you."

I followed Dixie to the display; she picked up a phone. "I'm getting one," I said. "Then we'll have something for emergencies and we can get rid of yours."

She held the package and muttered, "I'm not throwing out my phone," before handing it to me.

I paid for it and also for three refill cards, with probably more minutes than I'd ever use. The cashier set up the first card for me. "Good luck," she said when she handed it back.

We left the store and looked for a place we could get some clean clothes. As we walked, a guy came up behind us and started talking. "What do you need? I got smokes, I got smoke, I got rock, I got molly."

We didn't turn. I imagined that he had X-ray vision and could see straight into my backpack.

"I know it's early, ladies, but it looks like you have a long day ahead of you and you probably want a little help to get through it, right?"

Dixie held up her middle finger.

"Okay, okay, I can take a hint." He kept walking with us, then got in front and turned, walking backward. He wasn't much older than me. Seahawks knit cap, blond scruff on his face, baggy jeans. He looked back and forth between us. "You sisters?"

We didn't answer.

"Nice," he said with a laugh. "Nice."

"Could you fuck off?" Dixie said. She grabbed my arm and walked faster.

He followed us down the street for a while, talking dirty, until he got bored and went to bother someone else. Dixie pulled me into a drugstore; we looked at the cheap three-packs of underwear in pastels I'd never in my life seen on Dixie. "It covers her belly button," she said, pointing to the headless woman on the package. "I can't wear these."

"Who's going to see you, other than me?"

"That's not the point. The point of clothes is how you

feel in them. I don't want polyester grandma underwear bunching up around my ass, do you?"

"I guess not." I moved down the aisle and found a similar three-pack of T-shirts. I took it off the hook.

"No," Dixie said. "You will sweat like a pig in those and they also itch."

"Why did you bring us in here if you hate everything?"

"I don't know." She grabbed some tube socks and glanced down the aisle. "We should put the money in these," she whispered. "So it's not all loose in your bag. Come on."

We paid for the socks; then I followed her out and we walked up a few more blocks to a huge mall that Dixie had been to with Lia. The inside was all curving glass and soaring escalators and giant pillars holding it together. Dixie took me into one store, and after we found a few pairs of underwear she deemed cute enough for us, and one basic black T-shirt each, I checked the time. It was ten thirty. "We should get back down to the ferry terminal," I said.

"He's not going to find us here that fast." She was riffling through a rack of coats. "You need a new jacket."

"We said we wouldn't spend—"

"Oh fuck that. If he didn't want us spending the money, he shouldn't have left it in our room, I guess."

Like I'd been saying the whole time. I think she needed

to hear it in her own voice.

She made me try on not only jackets but jeans and shirts, too. Things that I thought looked good or at least fine, she frowned at and took away. She came in and out of the dressing room with new armloads of stuff to try.

We'd both always worn secondhand and cheap, but she knew how to put things together so they looked good. My clothes were jeans stretched out by other people's butts and knees, shirts where someone pulled on a thread and kept pulling. Sweaters . . . The sweaters were the worst. No matter how much you washed them or aired them out, they always smelled like Goodwill and the bodies of strangers. I'd tended to look like I was made of someone else's bad decisions, and I'd wished Dixie would help me, like she was helping me now.

When I pulled on what felt like the twentieth pair of stiff, dark jeans, she said, "Those."

"They're too long," I said.

"No, they're perfect." She knelt and cuffed the bottoms and turned me to face the mirror.

I looked tougher, older. More like her. "I don't know."

"They're perfect," she repeated. "But now you need boots."

Our eyes met in the mirror. "Dixie . . ."

"If you're going to disappear into the woods or whatever you're going to do, you need some good boots. And you're getting this sweater, too." She held up a hooded gray wool zip-up. A coat—a peacoat style but lighter weight—was already in our buy pile.

I didn't argue. What was a few hundred dollars out of almost thirty thousand anyway? While we were in the dressing room, we stuffed the bundles of money into the socks we'd bought at the drugstore, leaving out enough to pay for the clothes and a handful of money for each of us so we wouldn't have to dig into the backpack for every little thing.

That store didn't have shoes; we moved on. It was getting close to noon. "This has to be our last stop," I told Dixie when we went into a place with boots in the window.

Dixie tried on at least as many boots as I did. "Coming with me to the woods?" I said it like a joke, but I really wondered.

"The concrete jungle, maybe."

This time I chose for myself—boots that were dark brown suede, pull-on, a little higher than my ankle. They were lined, so they were soft and warm inside, but they had a rugged sole. I could see how they'd go with the new jeans and everything else, and I felt stable walking around.

"Those are good," Dixie said. "But you should try these on, too." She kicked another of the boxes toward me.

"No. I'm getting these."

She smiled, only slightly. "Okay, then." She picked out a pair of electric blue Doc Martens for herself. "I've been wanting these for like a year," she confessed.

I didn't even want to know the prices on what we'd gotten. Dixie went up to pay. Then we found a bathroom and changed into our new stuff in separate stalls. When I came out, I started to put the pair of jeans I'd left home in into my backpack, then thought, *no*.

"Throw it all away." I'd said it aloud.

Dixie watched me ball the jeans up, and the stretched-out Goodwill sweater, and my torn jacket, and finally I dumped my old shoes. I shoved it all deep into the bathroom trash can. She watched me check myself in the mirror, watched me see how different I looked. In black and gray, new denim and good wool. Without speaking, she stood behind me and combed her fingers through my hair. She twisted it around and pinned it back with bobby pins from her own hair, which now came loose.

Her touch was gentler than I'd come to expect from Dixie. I felt her breath on my neck when she said, "There."

"There," I echoed, staring straight into my eyes.

18.

ON THE walk from the store to the dock, I understood what Dixie meant about the point of clothes being how they made you feel. In the new clothes, I was a different person, solid on my legs. Strong. My face, with my hair back, felt exposed, like people could see all my flaws, all my angles. But it felt good to not hide, to not apologize for existing.

I hadn't been on a ferry since seventh grade, when my class took a trip to a marine park on one of the islands. Which island, I can't remember, or much about the park. I do remember standing up on deck with Miriam Reed when we were still friends, and the way birds would fly right next to the ferry, and the wind in my face, all of it making me feel a kind of freedom I never had before. This time, Dixie and I sat inside, on benches facing each other, near an electrical outlet. I kept my backpack snug between me and the large window while my new phone charged, and I sensed something like that same freedom, a space opening up inside me where I'd only felt smallness before.

It wasn't only me who noticed—Dixie kept staring. "Shit, Gem. You should see yourself." She took her charger out of her bag.

"How come you never helped me before when I asked? With clothes and stuff?"

"It's not just the clothes." She struggled with the packaging of the charger.

"Yeah, but—"

"I don't know," she said. "I guess I'm a selfish bitch?"

"I'm not saying that."

"I know. But are you going to be mad at me forever? For every time I wasn't who you wanted for a sister?"

It surprised me, that she saw it that way. "No. Are you?"

She suddenly dropped the package. "Fuck! Fucker." She'd torn off part of her fingernail; there was blood.

I resisted taking her hand to check the cut, like I might have before. "You used to like me," I said. "When you were little."

"Gem . . ." She cradled her hurt hand in the other. "Don't."

We had this time. We had this little bit of time together for being honest. It felt sharp and finite, like it could end any second without warning. "I know you want me to be different than I am," I said. "But you could have helped me be more what you wanted by actually talking to me. Telling me things."

She squeezed her finger. "I need to go get a paper towel."

She stalked off. A gull flew alongside the window, pumping its wings and moving at the same speed as the ferry, exactly like I remembered birds doing on that seventh-grade trip, as if it wanted to be close to the boat, the people. One of its eyes seemed to stare straight at me.

Maybe I could ride the ferry for days, getting on different ones and using the money a little bit at a time for food and shelter, if I needed it. Maybe I could last out here off and on ferries for . . . I don't know. Months? Would anyone notice me? Would anyone—Dad, Mom—even *look* for me? For reasons other than getting the money back, I mean.

The gull peeled off and flew up out of sight.

Dixie returned from the bathroom and picked up our conversation. "*You're* not exactly big on personal sharing, you know."

"I don't have anything to share."

She stared at me and then let out an incredulous laugh. "Okay. Your life is totally normal. I get to high school and find out you don't have friends, and you never told me that. You're in Bergstrom's office all the time and I have no idea what you talk about. You're a secret *smoker*. Yeah, nothing to see here, okay, Gem."

I unplugged my phone and put it, and the charger, in my bag. "Is your finger okay?"

"It hurts but yes."

"Let's go up on deck." I wanted to be in the wind and open air.

We shouldered our bags and climbed the steps. I held the rail to steady myself from the very slight rocking of the boat on the water. Strong in my boots and warm in my coat, I led Dixie to the front of the ferry. The wind blew harder than I expected, but I liked it—the sting on my face and the sense of steady movement, us gliding away from the city and the people we'd been there.

After a few minutes, we walked around to the back and leaned over to watch the foaming trail of water behind us.

"I lied," Dixie said. "About going on the Ferris wheel with Dad."

For a second I didn't understand what she was saying. I thought she meant she'd lied about not enjoying it because she hadn't wanted my feelings to get any more hurt than they already were.

"It never happened," she continued. "You want to know about me? I'm telling you." Her eyes had that Dixie defiance, ready for me to be mad at her.

I wasn't, though. I tried, but the resentment for her that I could usually find in a second wasn't there. How could I have been mad at Dixie so long for wanting exactly what I did? What anyone in our situation would want? Like she said, it wasn't her fault. Sometimes it was just hard to accept that things weren't how they should be.

Her hair blew around her face; her defiance had evaporated. I put my arm around her, half expecting her to shove me away. But she turned and fell into me and I held her, close. The way she cried at fourteen was different from how she'd cried at six. No big sobs. No drama. Just a quiet shaking and the pressure of her fingertips digging into my sides, my hands, stinging in the wind, pressed to her back.

She pulled away, red-eyed and blotchy. She swiped her sleeve across her nose. "I'm freezing."

We went back down and I managed to get her charger out of its package. Dixie plugged her phone in and we both stared at it as it came to life. One alert after another poured in—a stream of messages, a couple of voice mail notifications. Dad's texts alternated between angry and sorry.

answer your goddamn texts dix!!! this is IMPORTANT!
Then:
I'm not mad just call me
In another one he asked:
is gem with you??
It was the first mention of me since it all began.

There were also messages from Mom, who seemed to have no idea what was really going on; she'd only sent a check-in text to see how Dixie's night at Lia's was and if Dad had bothered her anymore. He'd come by the apartment, she said, but he wouldn't tell her what he wanted. She was working a shift at the bar tonight but she'd see us later.

"Listen to the voice mails," I said. "We should know what he's thinking."

"I don't *want* to know what he's thinking. I don't *care* what he's thinking. I don't want to hear his stupid fucking voice. If he tries calling again, there's no way I'm picking up." She jiggled her leg and stared out the window, then turned to me suddenly. "Let me see yours. Your phone."

I handed it over, and she started punching in numbers.

"What are you doing?"

"I'm adding contacts. Mom and Dad and Lia." She glanced up at me. "I don't know. We got this as backup, right? Just in case. Anyway, if they get your number somehow, don't you want to know it's them so you don't accidentally answer?"

"They're never going to get my number." If that happened, I'd do what the girl at the phone store said and get rid of it.

Dixie finished with it and handed it back. An announcement came over the ferry's loudspeaker that we'd be docking in five minutes; drivers should get back to their cars. My next decision was here and I had no idea what to do. "We need to listen to the voice mails," I said. I didn't like not knowing.

She nodded. "After we get off the ferry."

The other passengers collected their stuff and threw out their trash from the café and either went back to their cars or gathered at the pedestrian ramp. We sat still, charging her phone as much as we could until the last possible moment. Through the windows all around us the island drifted closer. Dixie fixed her gaze on the trees, the smaller boats that filled the harbor. It started to rain, fine drops hitting the Sound.

Dixie shook her head, then asked, "How come nothing good ever happens to us?"

I knew she didn't mean the rain.

19.

WE CAME off the ferry and Dixie went into the small terminal to use the bathroom.

I stayed outside. I flipped the hood of my sweater up to keep the drizzle off while I walked a little bit away from the terminal area for a better view, and to get farther from the exhaust of the ferry. I gazed up at the hills; they were covered in evergreens. Even in the rain—especially in the rain—it was beautiful. I thought of Dixie's joke about me living in the woods.

Why not? I mean, not camping, but maybe someday having a little cabin or cottage. It could be tiny—one room and a bathroom. I wouldn't be picky and I don't need a lot. And if I had the money, not just some but all of it . . .

I couldn't do this one day at a time forever, waiting for Dixie to figure out what she wanted to do. As if she had a choice. She wasn't even fifteen yet. Despite what Dixie said, I had a feeling my mom would let me go my own way; I'd be eighteen in a little less than a year anyway. She'd never let Dixie go that easily. If Dixie came with me, we wouldn't be starting a new life, we'd just be running and it wouldn't be a game, and I'd be responsible for her.

I couldn't do it. Everything I had to give, I needed to give to myself.

Dixie had to go home. And I had to make a real plan.

With the money on my back and Dixie in the bathroom and the ferry boarding for the return trip to Seattle, I thought: What better way to make sure Dixie didn't limit my options, didn't get scared into telling Dad where we were or give him the money, than for me to just . . . take it, and leave? That was my plan A to begin with, and here I was back in the same place, trying to decide if I was capable of going without saying good-bye to her, if I was capable of abandoning her.

She'll be okay, I told myself. She'd understand now. She had enough to get back, with the cash in her pocket left from all our shopping. I could get on the return ferry, that minute. When she figured out I'd left, she could get a ticket for the next one and go home and tell Dad whatever she wanted to tell him. I could lose myself somewhere on the Seattle side for a few hours or a day. Then ferry back over and, I don't know, hitchhike deeper into the island? Or go far away, to another state. By myself, responsible for only me.

Then I imagined her coming out of the bathroom, looking all over for me. I thought of her face when she asked why nothing good ever happens to us, and what she'd said about how she couldn't go home without the money. How betrayed she'd feel. How betrayed *I'd* feel, if I were her.

So I'd give her the backpack and send her home. I'd still have what I needed. I put my hands in my coat pockets, feeling for the phone, the Haciendas, the hotel washcloth—

My heart stopped.

No.

No!

I went over it in my mind again, and again, as if I would come to some other conclusion than that I'd thrown seven thousand dollars into the trash can in the mall bathroom, in the pocket of my old jacket. My head filled with a low buzzing as Dixie came back into view. I couldn't go back for it, not now, not without confessing to Dixie about secretly stashing money, lying to her. If it was even there anymore.

Dixie couldn't go home without the money; I couldn't leave without it. My backup plan, my safety net, was gone.

When she reached me, I could tell something was wrong.

"What happened?" I asked, trying to hide the horror I felt over my own carelessness.

"She's a fucking—" She mashed her lips together and turned away from me, striding fast back toward the water. She had her phone in her hand.

I jogged after her. "Who?"

"Fucking *Mom* is who," she said over her shoulder.

"Dixie, wait." She only walked faster. The voice mails. She must have listened to the voice mails when she was in the bathroom. "What did she say?"

She broke into a run straight toward the water and for a second I worried she'd climb the rail and jump in. But when she got right up to it, I knew exactly what she was doing.

She pulled her arm back, and the phone flew out of her hand in a huge arc in the gray sky before dropping into the Sound.

I got to her and touched her shoulder; she batted my hand away.

"Tell me what she said."

"Now *she* wants the money. Dad told her about it and now *she* wants me to come home with it."

"He told her?" I asked, confused. It was easy to imagine him using the idea of all this money to manipulate Mom, but harder to believe she'd fall for it, especially after the way she'd dumped all of the food.

"She only ever *wants* something from me," Dixie said through her tears. "She wants me to listen to her when she thinks she's in love or some guy breaks up with her. She wants me to get her pills from kids at school. She wants me to act like her fucking best friend but she doesn't ever do anything for me."

"What happened, though?" I was still fixated on the image of my jacket in the bathroom trash can, and Dixie was barely making sense. "All this was on a voice mail?"

"She called." She calmed down a little bit, taking deeper breaths. "I wasn't going to answer, but then I did, in case school called or something to say I'm not there. I wanted to give her some reason I—"

"You shouldn't have talked to her." It was too risky, what could come out in an emotional conversation.

Dixie dropped her arms. "Well, I did. And she was all, 'Do you have the money? I just talked to Dad and he says you have this money and oh Dixie you should bring it home, what do you think you're doing, we need it blah blah.'"

"Maybe she's just worried about you?"

"She didn't ask if I'm okay. Running around the city with this money. She *didn't even ask if I'm okay.* It was more like she's mad. Just really . . . *mad.*"

Of course she was mad, I thought. And Dixie'd never been able to handle Mom being mad at her. "Did you tell her you're with me?" I asked.

Dixie wiped her face with her sleeve. "I'm so stupid. Like you've been trying to tell me. Well, you were right, so you can be happy about that."

"I'm not." She'd already forgotten every single thing that had happened between us on the ferry.

"I told her to go to hell." She looked at me. "I should have told her *I* didn't even take the stupid money! None of this was even my idea."

"I know." I shifted on my feet. The new boots had started to rub my right little toe.

"I wish you'd left it there like you said you would. None of this would have happened." She wiped a tear away. "Everything was fine like it was."

"No it wasn't."

"For me it was."

We were back to where we'd started. There wasn't any point arguing about something she didn't want to see. I knelt down and opened the backpack to get out one of the spare packs of Haciendas I'd brought along. I needed to think, I needed one of my rituals back. I asked Dixie if she wanted one; she nodded.

We got two cigarettes lit in the drizzle, cupping our hands around the matches from the Velvet, and found a bench partly protected by a big tree with spreading branches. Dixie stared out at the water, quiet, forgetting to actually smoke while her ash got longer and longer. I tried words out in my head, tried to imagine what it would feel like to tell her what I'd done, losing a big chunk of the money.

"Can I get a smoke?"

The voice had sounded like a girl's, but when I looked up, I saw a guy around our age, in jeans and sneakers, coat and knit cap. A little bit of shaved head and a fuzz of light hair showed at the temples.

Dixie looked him—or her?—up and down, flicked her ash.

I handed over the pack.

"Are these Mexican?"

"Do you want one or not?" Dixie asked.

The person smiled. *Girl*, I thought again. "Can I get a light, too?"

I gave her my matchbook.

"Oh shit, matches. Can I just . . ." She held out her hand for my Hacienda and used it for a light, then gave it back. "Thanks."

We sat another few seconds. Then Dixie said, "Fuck. I can't keep this fucking thing lit in this fucking rain." She threw her half-smoked Hacienda on the ground and got up to walk closer to the water, her arms wrapped around herself.

The girl sat on the bench where Dixie had been. "You guys cutting school, too?" she asked.

"Not really. I mean, yeah, but . . ." I pointed across the Sound to the city. "I go to school over there." *Went to.*

"I wish I lived in the city. Nothing but assholes at my school."

"Oh."

"'*Oh*,'" she said with a laugh. "Yeah. I'm Kip."

"Gem. And there are plenty of assholes at my school, trust me."

"Is that short for something? Gemma? Jemima?"

"No. Gem like a diamond."

"What's up with her?" Kip asked, pointing with the cigarette to Dixie, whose back was still to us.

"She's my sister," I said, as if that answered the question.

Kip looked at me. "What's her name?"

"Dixie."

Dixie turned and came toward us. "I'm hungry and it's cold. What's the plan?"

"Finding lunch, I guess?"

Her eyes flicked to Kip. "Do you live here?"

"Yep." She dropped her cigarette and stepped on it with the heel of her sneaker. "There's a good diner nearby. If you like burgers and other dead animals and stuff."

"Can you show us where?" Dixie asked.

"Sure."

20.

THE DINER smelled like grease and meat, bacon and coffee and pancakes. There weren't a lot of people there; we were between lunch and dinnertime. It had been a short walk, a few blocks up from the harbor. A woman in jeans and a T-shirt and a green apron, hair dyed black and up in a bun, tattoos on her arms, greeted us. "Table or booth?"

"Booth," Kip answered.

The whole situation seemed like a bad idea to me. Every person who knew anything about us would be a risk. If not right away, then to me, later, if I had the money and Dad or Mom was looking. But it wasn't like I had an alternate plan to suggest, and I was preoccupied with how badly I'd screwed up, from the beginning. Maybe Dixie was right. Even if everything wasn't fine before, maybe it was better than whatever this was going to turn into.

She sat next to Kip on one side, their shoulders almost touching, and I sat on the other. There was a tin cup full of crayons, along with paper place mats to draw on.

"They have breakfast all day," Kip said.

"We've eaten a *ton* of food in the last twenty-four hours," Dixie said to Kip, holding her paper menu up. I could barely see her face. "I can't believe I'm hungry again."

I tried to make eyes at Dixie like, *Don't say so much.* She wouldn't look at me.

"Order anything you want," she continued, to Kip. "It's on us."

"I have money," Kip said.

"It's on us anyway."

My anxiety ticked up. I stared at my menu without seeing it.

"So, what's fun around here?" Dixie asked.

"Nothing."

Dixie laughed a strange laugh. Something about her had changed since we'd met Kip, and not only that she'd gotten cold toward me.

"On a nice day I go to this park on the other side of the

island. It's like a hundred acres. It has everything. Swings and slides. Trails. Ducks and stuff."

"Ducks! I love ducks."

I finally caught Dixie's eye. *You "love" ducks?*

"They're *funny*."

Kip laughed, and the waitress came back. I ordered a bacon cheeseburger and fries. Kip got vegetarian nachos and a shake. Dixie ordered a black bean burger and said to Kip, "I'll share mine if you share yours."

After the waitress left, Kip asked Dixie if she was a vegetarian.

"Pretty much," Dixie answered.

"No you're not," I said.

"How do *you* know?"

"From the salmon you ate last night? And the bacon mac and cheese?"

Her face got pink. "You're high," she said, shaking her head. She rested loosely on her elbows and whispered to Kip, loud enough—on purpose—for me to hear. "Gem lies. And steals."

She'd completely changed back to the Dixie I knew from before we found the money—ignoring me, ridiculing me, giving all her attention to someone she wanted to make like her. The part of me I'd let Dixie into for the last two days began to close up.

"I'm going to go wash my hands," I said, and scooted

out of the booth. When I picked up my backpack, Dixie said, "You can leave your stuff. We'll watch it."

"No thanks."

I was only in the bathroom a few seconds before Dixie came in behind me.

"What are you doing?" I asked her as I scrubbed the cigarette smell off my hands.

"Just making sure you don't crawl out a window with the money or something."

"No, back there." I turned off the water and hit the button on the hand dryer. "You love ducks? You're pretty much a vegetarian? Saying we're going to buy all the food? What do you think—"

Then a stall door opened and a woman with short gray hair came over to wash her hands. We immediately shut up and Dixie went into the other stall. I turned on my heel and left.

When I got back to the booth, Kip said, "You know what's funny?"

Nothing, I thought. *Nothing is funny.* "What?"

"I'm pretty sure your sister thinks I'm a dude."

Our eyes met and then it made sense. What Dixie had been doing. Flirting and lying and trying to seem impressive. We laughed, and I instantly felt the relief of not being alone.

"Should I tell her the truth?" Kip asked me.

I shrugged and put the backpack between me and the wall. "I don't care."

Kip glanced at the bathroom door. "I have a sister, too," she said. "And two brothers."

"Do you get along?"

"Uh, no. My sister is mad at me that I don't dress or act more like how she thinks a girl should, like I used to. This is kind of new," she said, pointing at herself. "A few months ago I had long hair and went around in yoga pants and dumb little tops, like my sister. People don't like it when you change." She took some sugar packets out of a bowl on the table and arranged them in a line, corners touching. "And my brothers are mad at me because they say I'm trying to be like them. Which, trust me, I'm not. Being like them is *not* on my list of life goals."

She moved the sugar packets into a circle.

"Dixie's mad at me because . . ." Because of our parents. Because of the money. Because of a million things, most of which had nothing to do with us. "We act mad at each other. But really it's other things."

Dixie came back from the bathroom. She'd cleaned off the smudges of makeup that had been under her eyes from crying, and fixed her hair a little bit. Kip and I shared another glance.

"What?" Dixie asked as she sat down, getting right up close to Kip again.

"Nothing."

The food came. Dixie kept taking nachos off Kip's plate like they were best friends, and shoving her fries at Kip. My burger was good but not as good as the one I'd had at the hotel.

"So, what's up with you guys anyway?" Kip asked. "Like, why are you on the island?"

Dixie said, "We're on the run."

I glared; she ignored me. "Just cutting," I said. "Taking a break."

Kip subtly slid her nacho plate a little farther away from Dixie.

"Gem basically kidnapped me," Dixie said. "She forced me onto a bus and made me lie to my mom and she's not going to let me go back unless I let her have something that isn't hers."

She wanted me to react, to *lose my shit*, as she would put it, to prove something to me or to herself. I made myself calm, counting something other than money for the first time since we'd left home. I chose the crayons. There were only eight; I could count and recount while talking. "We have some stuff going on at home," I said.

Kip nodded. "I'm going to have some stuff going on at home, too, if I don't get back soon. You guys want a ride somewhere? My car is parked down by the terminal."

Dixie looked at me. "Ask Gem. She's the one running

this show. I'm just a helpless victim."

I did another round with the crayons. "Is there a hotel around here we could get into with a fake ID and cash?" I stopped worrying about what Kip might think of us and money. For all she knew, we always had money. She probably had us pegged as spoiled rich kids, with our new clothes and paying for lunch and everything. I almost laughed at the idea.

Kip thought for a second. "Not a hotel. But a motel. You won't need me to drive you, we actually passed it on the way here." She took a green crayon out of the tin cup—I subtracted it, *seven*—and wrote her number on a corner of one of the paper place mats. "Call me if you guys need anything while you're out here." She tore the corner off and Dixie took it out of her hand even though I was pretty sure Kip had intended to give it to me.

We all stood and gathered our stuff, and Dixie paid at the counter. It had stopped raining and the cloud cover had broken apart, showing bright blue sky. "I know you said you wish you lived in the city," I told Kip as we walked down the hill, "but I think the island is beautiful."

"It is beautiful. And I hate it. I feel trapped, is the main thing, and people here don't get me."

"Why don't they get you?" Dixie asked.

Kip paused, then said, "Because I'm a girl who suddenly decided to dress like a boy but isn't gay. I'm just me."

Dixie stopped walking. Her cheeks were red as she stared at Kip.

"It's okay," Kip said. "It happens all the time, I don't care."

I knew Dixie cared, though. She started walking again, ahead of us but not far enough ahead that we could talk about her without her hearing, so we stayed quiet the rest of the way to the motel. When Kip said good-bye, she hugged me. Surprised, I stepped back.

"Sorry," she said. "I kind of hug everyone."

"It's okay. It's just that I kind of hug no one. Or more like no one hugs me."

"Seriously, you can call me if you need anything. And not that you asked for advice, but I'd be careful about staying on the island for too long. People here notice stuff quicker than they do over there." She nodded her head in the direction of the Seattle skyline.

Dixie had gone off to stand under the motel's car port.

"I guess she probably doesn't want a hug from me," Kip said with a laugh.

"Probably not."

Dixie took care of all the checking-in stuff, like last time. This place wasn't nearly as nice and didn't have room service and we only had to leave a hundred-dollar deposit. The guy acted like paying cash wasn't that unusual. His main concern—he said it twice—was that we not smoke in the room because then we'd have to pay an extra cleaning fee.

"We won't," Dixie assured him.

The room was plain and functional, with only a view of the parking lot behind the building. "Which bed do you want?" I asked Dixie.

"I don't care."

I dropped my stuff on the one closest to the door, same as the one I'd had at the nice hotel.

"I bet that was really funny to you," Dixie said.

"No."

"Did you know?"

"Yeah. I mean, I could tell right away."

Dixie unlaced her blue Docs and pulled them off her feet with a wince. "She says she's not gay but she was totally giving off the flirty vibe, right?" She stripped off her socks, her jeans, and her sweater, and sat on the other bed in her underwear and the black T-shirt.

I shrugged. "You're the one who gave off a vibe. It's like your automatic way of being when you're around guys."

"What? What do you mean? You never even see me around guys."

"Like Napoleon at the deli? Giving you sandwiches. And you get rides to school and I don't know what all else. You always have money."

"Are you calling me some kind of whore?"

"No. Forget it." I hung my new coat in the closet to dry, and my hoodie, too. I took off my boots and peeled off my socks; my little toe was red. I got my phone out. "Show me how to put Kip's number in here."

"Do it yourself."

"This phone is different than the one I had before. Anyway, you have it. The place mat."

She sighed and leaned over to pick her jeans up and dig in the pocket, then tried to throw the scrap of paper at me. It fluttered to the floor between the beds. I retrieved it and figured out how to save the number while Dixie turned on the TV and flipped channels.

"Why did you turn our problems into a joke like that?" I asked. "With Kip?"

"I didn't."

"Saying I kidnapped you and you're a victim and all of that."

"Maybe I am a victim. Maybe I should call the police." She wasn't going to do that and we both knew it. While she kept flipping through channels, never settling on anything, I stared at the ceiling, picturing the money I'd thrown out. Probably that bathroom garbage with my jacket in it had been emptied by now. Probably hours ago.

I'd have to let go of it. I'd have to let go of a lot of things.

"I'm sorry I let you keep thinking Kip was a guy," I told

Dixie. "I'm sorry for what Mom did to you."

"She didn't *do* anything to me," Dixie muttered.

"Well, you're mad at her. And taking it out on me. Like I was mad at Dad and taking it out on you. I'm sorry."

I rolled onto my side so I could see her.

"I don't want to do that anymore," I said.

"Do what?"

"Be mad at the wrong people."

I wished she'd say something, that it was okay or she understood. I wished we could talk, in a close way. She kept her eyes on the TV, though, and I rolled onto my back again.

I wondered if she'd ever forgive me for this whole mess. Everything that happened, it was only because we wanted our parents to be better, to know how to take care of us. We could at least try to forgive ourselves for wanting that.

21.

WE BOTH dozed off. I woke to the sound of rain pattering against our window. Before I opened my eyes, I couldn't be sure where I was, or when, or with who. I thought I could smell pine trees.

"Are you awake?" I asked, eyes still closed.

Dixie answered after a second. "Yeah."

"Do you remember that time we went camping with Mom and Roxanne?"

There was a long pause, and right when I'd given up on her answering, she said, "We had to eat those cold hot dogs all weekend."

Mom and Roxanne had wanted to get us out of the

house while Dad did a weekend detox. Roxanne borrowed a tent from one of her boyfriends and we drove in her beat-up hatchback to this camping place over two hours away, near Port Angeles. We walked the tide pools and Roxanne put a rough pink starfish in my hand. It undulated, mysterious and strange, against my skin. At night, Mom and Roxanne tried to get a fire started so we could cook out, but they didn't know what they were doing and the wood never caught.

I opened my eyes. "What else do you remember?" I asked.

"Cold marshmallows and Hershey bars and graham crackers."

Deconstructed s'mores, Roxanne had called them, after we tried and failed to roast the marshmallows over her lighter.

"What else?" I asked, turning to see Dixie. "Not only about that trip. About anything else. About us. Good things."

She rolled over, too, so we faced each other. Her hands were tucked under her cheek. That's how she'd lie when I'd read to her before she could read on her own. "I remember going to a school recital that you sang in. I was little. Mom and Dad took me to hear you."

I'd forgotten that. It was probably second or third grade. My teacher that year believed in the importance of music for "at-risk" kids, and didn't seem to think twice before calling us that to our faces.

"You could sing, Gem."

"Really?" I'd had a short solo. Something from the musical *Annie*.

"Yeah, you were good. Dad had me on his lap and he said to Mom, 'She can sing.'"

I tried to remember if he'd said it to me. "Are you making that up?"

"No!" Dixie laughed, then suddenly stopped. "No. I know I lied about the Ferris wheel, but I wouldn't lie about this."

"I never did any singing after that, though. I wonder what kinds of stuff we would have done if Mom and Dad hadn't been . . . like they were," I said. "Don't you wonder? Maybe I'd be doing school plays. Maybe you'd be in a band."

She smirked. "What would I play?"

"I picture you as a lead singer."

"I was thinking tambourine." She propped herself up to see the clock on the nightstand between the beds. It was a little after four thirty. We'd napped for maybe an hour. Dad was probably leaving more messages on Dixie's phone. I imagined the screen lighting up somewhere at the bottom of the Sound.

Dixie moved to a sitting position at the edge of her

bed and stretched her arms overhead. The nap seemed to have erased our fight about Kip and everything else, and I didn't want to mess with the fragile peace. Especially since in the back of my mind I knew this would probably have to be our last day together. I would take more money out of the backpack, or find a way to disappear with the whole thing.

She got up and walked across the room in her underwear, then bent over to get a dry shirt out of her bag. I watched her, and was surprised by something I'd never seen before.

"Is that a *tattoo*?"

"Oh. Yeah," she said.

"When did you get that?"

"The day after I got my fake ID. That was another reason I wanted one."

"Can I see?"

She came over to me with an armful of clothes and turned her back. I lifted her shirt. It was a star, just a simple star, above the back of her left hip. I touched it.

"Don't tickle me."

"You used to draw stars just like this all the time, on your notebooks, and around our heads whenever you drew us. Remember?"

"I guess."

"Did it hurt?" How had I not noticed it before, sharing a room like we did? She must have been trying to keep me from seeing.

There was so much I didn't know about her. Like if she'd had a real boyfriend, or if she'd had sex or done drugs—like the kind of drugs she'd brought home for Mom or anything else. I didn't know what she did at night when she wasn't home, what her friendship with Lia meant to her. It felt urgent, now, to find out everything, but I also knew it was probably too late. It made me sad, the idea that for the last few years I'd stopped knowing my sister, who she had become.

"Yeah, it hurt a little," she said. She stepped away from me and pulled on a new pair of leggings after ripping off the tag. "A tattoo like this just takes like ten minutes; it's over fast."

I watched her finish getting dressed. "How much did it cost?"

"I don't remember. Not a lot."

"I want one," I said. "A matching one."

She blew out a little laugh, as if I'd never really do it.

I reached for the new phone. "Maybe Kip knows a place around here we could go."

"You want to do it right *now*?" Dixie asked.

"I'll chicken out if I don't just go. You know how I am."

She shrugged. "Okay."

"You're coming, too. I want mine to be just like yours. They need to see."

"It's a star. It's not like it's the Mona Lisa or something."

"Come on," I pleaded.

There was a little bit of risk leaving her alone at the hotel. I'd take the phone and the money with me, but she could call Dad or Mom if she could remember their numbers. They could get over to the island within a couple hours and be waiting for me.

But that wasn't the reason I wanted her to come. At least, not the whole reason. "I need you there," I said. "For support. I want to do it together."

She studied me, then gave a small nod.

Kip knew a place over on the other side of the island that wouldn't card me, and said she could come pick us up. As soon as we got in the car, Kip said to Dixie, "Sorry about how I didn't just tell you right away, before, that I'm . . . me."

Dixie climbed in the backseat. "It was dumb," she muttered. "I should have figured it out."

We drove farther into the island. Apart from the sound of Kip's car, things were still and quiet. And green. So many trees lined the road that it seemed like the sun itself was beaming emerald and jade from its low position behind us. We passed a woman on a bicycle that had swooping lines and a big seat and a basket on the back. The handlebars had streamers. The woman's dark hair, gathered in a ponytail, flew behind her as she pedaled.

I twisted in my seat so I could see her until we went around a corner.

That could be me, I thought. *I could get a bike to ride around the island and put groceries or whatever in the basket.*

" . . . come to the city," Dixie was saying to Kip. She'd leaned forward to rest her chin on the front passenger seat. "I can take you to the best places. Our dad is gonna open a club. . . ."

Her saying that, those same old words, didn't do anything to me then. It didn't make me anxious or angry or jealous, not anymore. The space in me kept opening and the green light that surrounded the car seemed to fill that space. While she talked about her imagined future, I thought about my own.

I'd never thought much before about having a future. When Mr. Bergstrom would ask me about my plans after high school, I'd say *I don't know,* I'd say *Stop asking,* I'd change the subject. I couldn't see beyond the walls of our apartment or the few miles between home and school. Every day was about getting through it. Every weekend was about getting back to school, where there could be some structure and my routines.

It's not that I didn't want to see possibilities for myself. But I couldn't. I couldn't see how or where I'd wind up. I knew it couldn't be the same as Mom and Dad, but I didn't see exactly how it could be different from them and the whole twisted root system of our family tree.

And then I did see, in that moment. In the light, in the air, in the order and the disorder and Kip's noisy car and the woman on the bicycle. I don't know how or why right then—but I saw. I could belong in the world. There was space for me.

22.

THE TATTOO place was small, with every inch of its walls covered by pictures of tattoo designs. There was only one person working there, a middle-aged guy with a huge mustache and a black snake tattoo that wound around his neck and disappeared under the collar of his flannel shirt. If I'd seen him on the street, I'd have walked the other way, but here he didn't look out of place, and he was nice. Just like Kip said, he didn't even ask for ID.

Dixie showed him her tattoo and he looked at me and asked, "Is that all you want?"

"Yeah," I said. "But somewhere I can see it." I pulled up the sleeve of my hoodie and showed my forearm. "Here?"

He tapped closer to the inside of my elbow. His hands were covered in inked vines. "Up here is good. You can see it, but you can also hide it, like if you're at a job interview or something."

Kip had wandered off to look through a binder of more tattoo art. She'd told us on the way there she secretly had her own—a red balloon—on her shoulder and was thinking of getting another one.

"Let me trace yours and I'll make a stencil," the guy said to Dixie. "I'm Elton, by the way. I guess I should introduce myself before I go touching you."

I looked at Dixie's star while Elton made the stencil. It was so plain and alone. I wanted to mark myself to remember these days with her, but she was going to leave this place the same as when she got here.

I scanned designs on the walls. One was of two hearts linked together, sort of overlapping.

"Dixie," I said. "What if we did something like that?" I pointed. "Only with stars. Interlocking stars."

"Like add one to hers and put two on you?" Elton asked. "I like it. Want me to go draw something up? So you can see how it would look?"

Dixie pulled her shirt down. I waited for her to say no, that my idea was dumb or what would make me think she'd get a tattoo for me—something representing *us*—permanently on her body?

"Go ahead," she told Elton, and I smiled.

We sat with Kip on the bench and waited. "Are you going to do one?" I asked her.

"Not tonight. I have to think about it more."

Next to me, Dixie sniffled, and I looked in time to see her brushing a tear away.

"Are you all right?" I asked.

She lifted her shoulders in a shrug and again wiped her hand across her face.

Elton came back and brought over his stencils. One with two interlocking stars for me, and another with just one that he could lay over Dixie's existing tattoo to match. He'd added a little shading to both.

"That's awesome," Kip said.

I loved it. I wanted Dixie to love it, and to say so, and smile at me and hug me. All she did was nod and say "Okay," and it was almost enough.

Kip got up. "I'm going to take a walk."

"You can stay," I said.

"There's a bookstore near here I want to check out. I'll be back."

We paid cash up front, then he did mine first. I took off my hoodie and he cleaned my arm and shaved some of the fine hairs there. He used the stencil to position the design and transfer an outline to follow. "You sure that's exactly how you want it? Because this is forever."

I nodded.

Dixie sat with me. We were both mesmerized, by how the needle left ink on my skin and by the high buzzing of the gun. It didn't really hurt. Just enough for you to know something was happening to you. Elton worked fast—he was already moving on to the second star when I glanced at Dixie and saw tears in her eyes again.

"What?" I asked quietly.

"Nothing."

When Elton finished mine, he cleaned everything up and wrapped my arm in plastic and told me how to take care of it. "You guys can take a walk around the block if you want while I clean everything and set up for you," he said, nodding at Dixie.

We went out and I took the pack of Haciendas from my bag. "You want a smoke?" I asked Dixie. She shook her head and I realized I didn't want one, either.

She wasn't crying anymore but she didn't seem herself. My arm felt bruised. "It kind of hurts now," I said.

"Yeah, it'll be like that for a few days."

We walked down the street. It was dark by then except for streetlights, and colder than it had been the night before. Dixie wrapped her arms around herself, shivering. "Don't you think Mom is probably worried for real now?" she asked. "Like, reporting us missing?"

"Maybe."

"I don't want her to worry. We should call just to say don't worry. From Elton's phone or something so she can't get the number of yours."

It was like she had a kind of amnesia. About how mad she'd been about Mom earlier, after their phone call. And how obvious it was our parents weren't worried about us. Dad wanted the money, Mom wanted the money. Maybe they wanted us, too, but neither of them would want to have to explain the money to anyone like police.

"We're probably going to be on the news tomorrow," Dixie continued. "Our pictures will be around, so it will be harder to stay hidden. If we call her, maybe she won't report it. If she hasn't already, which she probably has."

She waited for me to say something.

"Maybe."

We'd walked around the whole block and were back to the tattoo place. Without speaking, Dixie went in and climbed onto the table and pulled her shirt up and the waist of her jeans down. She rested her head on her folded arms, with her face away from me.

Afterward we waited outside for Kip. I wanted Dixie to talk. About how she was feeling, or maybe to say that it meant something that we had matching tattoos now. All I got was the back of her head, then her annoyed face when she turned to ask, "Where the fuck is she?"

A minute later Kip's car rolled up. "Hey," Kip said.

Dixie yanked the door open and climbed into the backseat; I settled into the front, holding my backpack on my lap.

"You guys want to go to a party?" Kip asked.

"No," I said.

"What kind of a party?" Dixie asked.

"A party." Kip cranked up the windshield defrost and looked at Dixie in the rearview mirror.

"Not if it's, like, five people sitting around smoking a bowl and talking about five other people that we don't know."

Kip turned around in her seat and stared at Dixie. "You like to have things your way, I noticed."

Dixie stared back. "Doesn't everybody?"

"It's not going to be five people sitting around smoking a bowl. It should be pretty big. Everyone knows each other here. Music and snacks and probably whatever you want to drink."

"I thought you said your school was all assholes," Dixie said.

"I was in a mood. Anyway, even if they are, they're the only people I know and I get bored. So." Kip hit my thigh lightly with the back of her hand. "Do you want to?"

"We should get back to the motel," I said. I touched my wrapped arm. It was tender. I was tired. I needed rest so

I could leave in the night, if that's what I decided to do.

"You can go back," Dixie said. "I'm going to the party."

Maybe it was an opportunity—I could ask Kip to drop me off, send Dixie to the party with her. But when Kip pulled the car out onto the road, she said, "I'm only taking you if Gem comes."

"That's bullshit."

We drove a short way. It was one more thing we could do together. Then, then for sure, I could make a move. "Fine," I said. "I'll go."

We went back in the direction of the motel for about fifteen minutes. Kip pointed. "That's where I live. Down that street."

It was dark and we went by it too fast to see, but I got an impression of arching trees and fenced-in front yards. It was the kind of street I wouldn't mind living on someday. I only pictured myself, alone. Not with a husband and not with children, not even with a roommate. Just me. Quiet mornings and peaceful evenings and a fenced-in front yard.

Kip made a turn off the main road, and another turn, and slowed. "Parking is gonna suck." She glanced at me. "If you have like five bucks, throw that in the vase or whatever when you go in. To help with the snacks and drinks."

Dixie laughed. "Yeah, we have five bucks."

When we finally parked and Kip got out, I turned to

Dixie. "Don't say anything to anyone about us or what we're doing here. Just say we know Kip from . . . through our parents or something."

"I'm not an idiot."

I got out, and as I pulled my backpack onto my shoulder, it brushed against my tattoo. I winced.

Kip noticed. "You need some Advil or something?"

"If there is any."

"So you're supposed to know us through our parents or some shit," Dixie said to Kip.

"Plausible. My parents know a lot of people."

When we got in sight of the house where the party was, Dixie strode ahead of us straight for the front door, where some kids were crowding through and light shone out.

Kip turned to me. "What happened? You guys were kind of getting along for a minute in the tattoo place."

"Yeah," I said. "We were."

23.

AS WE walked in, I caught a glimpse of myself in the entryway mirror and remembered I had on my new clothes and this is how people would see me. This is how Kip saw me. A little tough, a little badass. A girl that just got a tattoo. The truth, though, was it was my first party—the first one since cake-and-ice-cream parties from childhood.

A big pottery bowl in the hallway overflowed with dollar bills. I threw in a five.

"People usually put their coats and stuff in one of the bedrooms, if you want to keep your backpack in there."

"That's okay." I craned to try to see where Dixie had

gone, but she'd already disappeared into the house. I looked back at Kip to ask where a bathroom was. I could take one of the sockfulls of money and put it in my pocket.

She grabbed my arm and pulled me down the hall. "Come on. Let's get a drink. Do you drink?"

"I . . . No."

"There's water and soda and stuff. Just have whatever you want. Don't worry, I won't desert you. I know it's weird to be at a party where you don't know anyone."

She brought me into the huge living room, where most of the people were. It wasn't like I'd always imagined this kind of party would be. The music wasn't blasting loud, people weren't shouting and dancing with their hands up. I guess all I knew about parties was from movies, which seemed to have it completely wrong. This was just a room full of people hanging out, talking and laughing.

A girl with long blond hair, wearing jeans and a pink sweater, spotted Kip and came straight over. "Where have you been all day? Mom is pissed." I studied her face; she and Kip looked exactly alike, more than regular sisters do. They must have been twins.

"It's not your problem," Kip said. "This is Gem."

"It is my problem when I'm the one who ends up making excuses for you, and by the way I don't enjoy that at all." She thrust her hand out. "Hi. I'm Jessa. There's a keg in the backyard if you want a beer. Other stuff in the kitchen," she said, pointing. To Kip she said, "Jeremy and Jonathan are here, too. Consider yourself warned."

"Great."

"Come find me before you leave." Jessa smiled at me. "Nice to meet you. Don't drink the punch unless you want to forget everything that happens tonight."

She skipped off toward the keg.

"Jeremy and Jonathan?"

"Our brothers. Yes, they're twins, too. Freshmen in college, so they're pathetic for being here." Embarrassed, Kip glanced at me. "My real first name is Julia." She waited. Then: "Get it? Julia, Jessa, Jeremy, Jonathan? It's horrible. Our parents are also both twins. My dad's name is Mike and his twin is Matt. My mom and aunt: Allison and Amanda. It's a generational disorder, the naming thing. My middle name is Kipling, my grandmother's maiden name. So. Kip."

"I like Kip," I said.

"I'm never having kids. There's like a hundred-and-twenty-percent chance I'd have twins, too. No way. Let's get some food."

I followed her to the kitchen. We loaded up paper plates with little mountains of chips and crackers and cheese. "Who brought celery sticks?" she asked a guy filling a glass with water at the sink. "Who brings celery sticks to a party?"

"Your *brother*," he said after he'd turned around.

Kip rolled her eyes. "Jeremy. He's on this paleo thing to make weight for wrestling."

The guy drank his water and looked at me, and didn't turn away. Did I seem weird? He didn't have the expression on his face people get when they think I'm weird. His hair was dark; he was big. Big and tall. I said hi. Then he asked Kip, "Where were you today? You missed that huge test in geometry."

"Yeeeaaah, I guess I kind of didn't want to take that. Anyway," she said, "these old friends of my parents are in town, so I had to show their daughters around." She looked at me. "They're practically like my cousins."

"What's your name?"

"Gem," I said.

"Jen?"

"Gem," Kip said. "Like a diamond."

"Nice. I'm Sefa," he said.

"She just got her first tattoo. Look." She put her plate down and took my arm and slid my sweater sleeve up gently. The stars, through the plastic wrap, were deep black against my reddening skin.

Sefa came closer, loomed. I felt small next to him and not sure I wanted to show anyone my tattoo yet. "Did it hurt?" he asked.

"Not too much. It hurts more now."

"Want some punch? You'll feel better."

Kip and I exchanged a glance; she smirked.

"No thanks." I pulled my sleeve down. "I need to find my sister."

"I'm gonna get you something for your arm," Kip said. "I'll look for you in a minute."

I left my cheese and crackers behind and went back out into the hall, adjusting the backpack on my shoulder, wondering which door led to a bathroom. Then I felt someone tugging on the backpack. I whipped around to see Sefa close behind me.

"Whoa," he said after my fast reaction. "Sorry. Just saying hi."

"I need to find my sister," I said again.

"That's cool," he said. "I'm not following you, just going in the same direction you are because that's where I'm going, so don't worry about it. I'll stay three feet behind."

"I know, I—"

"You look a little freaked out."

"I'm not."

I walked outside; Sefa went to the keg. Dixie was sitting in a corner of the yard, drinking out of a red plastic cup, with some guy. Sitting close like she'd sat close to Kip when they first met. While I watched, she handed him her cup to hold and shifted so she could lift the back of her shirt. Showing her tattoo.

I went over. "It matches mine," I said. I pulled up my sleeve to show the guy.

"Cool." His eyes flicked to mine. "You're the sister."

The sister. "What's she telling you?" I asked.

He shrugged and smiled in a way I didn't like. I looked into the cup Dixie had been drinking out of. "Is that the punch?" I asked.

"It's beer," Dixie said. "Did you want something?"

"I think we should leave soon." I'd never seen Dixie drink and I didn't know how she'd be. Thinking about how Mom and Dad were with it, I got anxious, and my instinct was to get her away.

Dixie took her beer back from him. "We literally *just* got here."

"Stay. I'll give you a ride home," the guy said to Dixie.

"Yeah," Dixie said to me. "I'll go with Ryan." She scooted closer to him and stared at me.

"Can I talk to you for a second?"

She shook her head. "No. You can't."

I moved toward her. As if I could take her arm and drag her away, as if she were six years old.

"You should show Ryan what's in your backpack, Gem." She leaned on him. I stopped moving. "There's like thirty thousand dollars in there. Approximately."

Ryan laughed like Dixie had made a joke. I laughed, too, a forced laugh. Dixie held my eyes intensely.

"Right," I said. I patted the shoulder strap. "Me and my piles of money."

"Half of it should actually be mine," Dixie told Ryan. "Sort of like an inheritance."

I tried to understand what she was doing. Her tears at the tattoo place. Messing with me now, knowing I wouldn't find it funny. Why she was saying the things she was saying, in front of everyone. And how angry she seemed, how hurt. *She's mad at Mom and Dad*, I reminded myself, *for using her, trying to control her to get what they want.*

I stared back at her, as hard as she stared at me, except what I wanted—what I'd always wanted—was to see myself through her eyes. This time, though, it wasn't to know how good I was, how needed I was. It was to see truth, for once.

Maybe she wasn't mad at the wrong people. Maybe she was actually mad at me, and maybe she was right to be. Maybe that was the truth. Or part of it.

Kip appeared next to me and held out her hand. There were three pills in it. "Ibuprofen."

I put them in my mouth and reached for Dixie's beer cup. She let me take it, still exposing me with her stare while I took a swallow to wash down the pills. I'd never tasted beer or any other alcohol—it was bitter and disgusting, like drinking vomit, but I made myself not show it on my face as I handed the cup back to Dixie.

Then I slid the backpack off and put it at her feet. "You can have it."

Finally she blinked. She looked down at it, then back up at me. I could see her trying to work out what was going on in my head or maybe in her own head. She tapped it with her blue Doc. "I don't want to lug your shit around."

Kip said, "Just put it in the room with all the coats."

"Let's go buy a car," Ryan joked.

"It's not for you," I said to him.

Ryan reached for the backpack. "Is there really money in here?"

"What?" Kip asked, confused.

"Don't touch that," I said.

Dixie nudged it away from him with her boot. "If by 'money' you mean Gem's dirty laundry, then yeah." I could hear a slight tremble in her voice that no one but me would catch. She kicked it back toward me. "I don't want this."

I swallowed. "Watch it for me. I'm going to go have a smoke." I turned to Kip. "Do you want one?"

"Gem," Dixie said, "wait." She stood and picked up the backpack.

"I'm just going for a walk," I said. "I'll see you later."

Ryan pulled her down onto his lap and laced his fingers around her waist. Kip took my arm and we left.

* * *

"These are the worst cigarettes I've ever tasted, by the way," Kip said after we both got our Haciendas lit. We were halfway down the block, away from the party. This street, like the one Kip said she lived on, had canopies of trees budding with new leaves.

"Oh." I didn't know cigarettes tasted any other way but bad. "They were my dad's." It felt strange, walking without anything on my back. My body was light, as if I could float up off the ground if I let myself.

"Were?"

"He's alive and everything. I took them after he moved out, so now they're mine."

She flicked hers to the ground after only a few drags. "What's going on with you and Dixie?" We turned a corner and saw the moon, a slim crescent. "Not that you have to tell me."

It was a story impossible to tell unless I started at the beginning. And I wasn't even sure where the beginning was. "It's complicated" was all I could say. We turned another corner and now we were facing the wind. My Hacienda went out; I tossed it into the gutter.

"She seems like a pain in the ass. And not that bright, either, if she's hanging all over a guy like Ryan after knowing him for two seconds."

I stopped walking and put my hands in my pockets,

gripping the fabric inside. "She's not stupid."

Kip stopped, too, and shrugged. "Okay. Well, you know her better than I do. Those are my first impressions and I only mean—"

"We've been through a lot. She does what she has to do. I do what I have to do."

"I didn't mean anything," Kip said, laughing as she gripped my shoulders. "I thought you needed to vent. But if what you want to do is stick up for her, then you don't need to vent and we can go back to the party and have fun."

I couldn't talk. I didn't want to move, to go back to the party or not go. This was my whole problem, being stuck for one reason or another. I opened my hands in my pockets and tried to draw a deep breath, but I couldn't.

Her grip on my shoulders loosened into something more gentle. "Are you about to cry?"

I shook my head.

"I'm sorry if I said something wrong," Kip said. "I know I don't really know you. I didn't want to piss you off or anything. I thought that's what you wanted, someone to take your side."

I forced breath in. "You have a big family. Your parents pay attention, right? Like they know when you come and go and where you basically are." I pointed over my shoulder. "Practically your whole family is at that party."

Kip nodded.

"Dixie's all I have. We only have each other. She's my sister. She's my little sister."

"Okay, I get it. I'm sorry," she repeated.

I stepped back from her and wiped my coat sleeve across my face. "She's the only one who knows."

Kip must have thought I meant some specific piece of information, some big secret, because she asked, "Knows what?"

To me, the answer was obvious: "What it's like to be us."

24.

WHEN WE got back to the party, Dixie was gone.

Kip and I checked all over the house, and I braced myself in case we walked in on Dixie and Ryan doing something I didn't want to see. They weren't in any of the rooms. In the one where people had tossed their stuff, I dug through the coats, checked under the bed and in the closet, looking for the backpack, just in case.

Then one of Kip's brothers told us Ryan and Dixie had taken off right after we went for our walk. "Where?" Kip said.

"I didn't know it was my job to ask," he said, holding his hands up. "I don't even know who she is." He had the same nose as Kip and Jessa, small and flat.

I could see Kip about to yell at him. I stopped her and said, "It's okay. Maybe you could take me back to the motel now."

People had stopped their conversations to watch us.

"If you want," Kip said.

Her brother dropped his hands. "Sorry," he said to me.

We went out to the car, silent. Then, while she was letting the defroster clear the windshield, she said, "I don't think you need to worry about her. Ryan's your basic dickhead but he's not dangerous."

"I'm not worried about that. She's always been able to handle herself with guys. That's not something I'd be able to help her with anyway. Don't know anything about it."

"Yeah, me neither. Well, not much." Impatient with the defroster, Kip swiped her arm across the last bit of fog and drove down the block.

I was thinking about what I'd done, leaving the money with Dixie. If I regretted it. Maybe it was stupid. But maybe there were some things worse than being stupid.

Kip turned onto the main road. "Do you want to go look for her? Do you want to call her?"

"She doesn't have a phone." Well, she did. My phone, the burner, was in the backpack. But I didn't have the number memorized.

"I can probably get Ryan's number from Jessa."

"No," I said. "Could you take me back to the motel?" Dixie would turn up there eventually. Or she wouldn't, and then I'd decide what to do next.

"Yeah."

"I'm tired. We . . ." I looked at her. "You probably figured out we left home."

"Kinda. I thought maybe."

"Have you ever done that?"

She shook her head. "No."

"Have you wanted to?"

She laughed. "Not for more than a few hours." We drove a bit farther. "Did you leave forever? Are you runaways now?"

That didn't seem like the right word for us. For me. I don't think I wanted to run away from something so much as find something else. "If we are, we're not very good at it," I said. "We're probably not even ten miles away from home."

"Why'd you leave? You said your Dad was gone. Do you have an asshole stepdad or something? Is your mom really strict?" She glanced at me. "Is it, like, abuse and stuff?"

"No. It's . . . I don't know. It's not great. A lot could be better." I thought about how back in the hotel Dixie had said maybe things hadn't been fine for me, but they were for her. Maybe that was only something she told herself, or it could be a little bit true. It was hard to explain to Kip without telling about the money. If it hadn't been for the money, we'd still be there. "It's always affected me more than Dixie," I said. "The stuff at home."

"Because you're older. The older ones always deal with more shit, or so my brothers say."

"That's part of it. I've always been different, though, from her. Sometimes I think she's mad at me because I'm not more like her."

"Maybe she's mad at herself that she's not more like *you*," Kip said. "I feel that way sometimes. Like why couldn't I be happy being part of 'Julia and Jessa'? It was easier. It wasn't me, though. I didn't want to be one of those people who goes her whole life not being herself."

Kip talked more about deciding to cut her hair, change her name, change her clothes, but I got fixed on what she'd said about Dixie being mad at herself for not being like me. Could that be true even a little bit? I couldn't imagine how. Dixie had friends, Dixie was cute, Dixie got along better with Mom and Dad. What was there about me to like? To want?

We were at the motel. "Are you sure you'll be okay?" Kip asked. "Do you want me to go in with you and see if she's there? If you want me to get Ryan's number—"

"No. I'm fine." I pushed the car door open, caught up in my own thoughts, but before I could get out, Kip grabbed my arm. I looked back at her.

"Um, good-bye?" she said. "I mean, you're not just going to get out of the car and slam it in my face after I drove you all around today and everything."

"Oh." I reached into my jacket pocket. "I could give you some gas money. . . ."

Kip laughed, then just sat there with her face turned to me. I couldn't see her eyes too well in the car but she didn't seem mad. "We're friends, Gem. Don't worry about it. But don't jump out of my car without saying good-bye."

"Thank you," I said. "Thanks."

"Call me if you need help. Call me if you don't. Text me or whatever. Stay in touch. Let me know what happens."

"Yeah. I will. Bye."

She leaned over and hugged me. I got out and watched her drive off. I waved.

When I went up to the room, Dixie wasn't there but her stuff was. Not that her stuff was anything she would need to come back for. She was wearing her new clothes, her boots.

I turned off the light and lay on the bed.

I could hear the TV in the room on the other side of the wall. And sometimes passing headlights would beam moving light onto the ceiling. The heater fan rumbled on and shuddered off at random intervals; it made my muscles tense up every time.

But I was all alone.

This is what it's like without Dixie, I told myself.

I'd slept alone before. There were all those times she'd spent the night somewhere else. And then there were all the ways she made me invisible to her at school, and all the ways she ignored me at home. There were the times she yelled at me to leave her alone, or gave me the silent treatment. But there's a way a person is *there* even when they aren't and even when they don't want to be. A way a sister is there.

That night, though, I knew she could be gone. Really gone. Because she'd told me from the beginning she wouldn't go back without the money, and then I gave it to her. Most of it, anyway. I might as well have said *Go home.*

I let that idea, of her going back and me going forward, sink way down into my heart and pump through me with my blood. The way Kip wasn't part of Julia and Jessa anymore—what if I wasn't part of Gem and Dixie? Would I still be me? Kip talked about wanting to be herself, but I couldn't think who I was without Dixie to take care of, or Dixie to avoid, or Dixie to be mad at. Dixie to feel hurt by, Dixie to feel jealous of.

I made an image of myself in my mind. Walking on a road, in the clothes Dixie had chosen for me. Me, putting one boot in front of the other, moving forward, forward, with my back to whoever could see me, whoever was watching.

And I realized it was Dixie. Dixie was the one watching, the one whose eyes I saw myself through as I walked away.

25.

I FELL asleep for a couple of hours and woke up with a stiff neck and a growling stomach. My arm throbbed. I wished I'd thought to get a few more pills from Kip, also that I'd eaten more at the party or at least stuffed some cheese cubes into my pockets.

Dixie hadn't come back.

Yet, I thought, almost as a reflex. Still, I had to start figuring out what I would do after I checked out of the motel at noon—eleven hours away. Where could I go next? I had less than two hundred dollars left of what we'd doled out to ourselves in the dressing room. This wasn't a game. Either I had to go home, or this was my life now.

And I wasn't going home.

I moved in the dark to the little desk with the phone and clicked on the light, sat in the wheeled chair. The phone had buttons for the front desk and for emergencies. The instruction card next to it detailed the prices for personal calls and how they'd be added to your bill when you checked out. Halfway through doing the math, I realized how dumb I was being. My problem wasn't the cost. My problem was that the phone was for people who had someone to call, friends or family or connections, people they could rely on.

I tried. I thought about Roxanne. I think she would have driven out to get me if she knew I was in trouble, even though she hadn't seen me for years. She wouldn't invite me to move in with her or anything, but she'd come for me at the very least. She might talk me through this. Only I didn't know her number or if she even lived in the area anymore. I picked up the phone and called information even though it was going to cost me over two dollars, according to the price list.

"What city?" the operator asked.

"Seattle. I think."

"Name?"

"Gem," I said automatically.

"That a last name? Spell it?"

Then I realized he meant he needed the name of the

person I was trying to reach. "I . . . I don't know the last name."

He paused. "Is this a prank?"

"No," I said quickly. "No." Roxanne was always just Roxanne. If she or Mom ever said her last name, I didn't remember it. "Can you look up first names? Roxanne? It's not that common."

"Honey . . ." I heard a sigh, then a typing noise. "Hang on. Roxanne Adams. Roxanne Chang. Roxanne Crandall. Roxanne Evans. Roxanne Fletcher, Roxanne Fung, Roxanne George, Roxanne Granger—two of those, believe it or not. Roxanne Gunderson. Roxanne Haverford. Roxanne—"

"Never mind." I didn't know her name and I wasn't going to suddenly know it. "What about . . . Idaho. Ivan Kostas."

"You know the city?"

"No."

He started to say something else but I hung up. The things in the world made to help people weren't going to help people like me.

Imagine:

Your family is broken. Your family is addicted. Your family is poor or sick or unstable in some other way, and your family doesn't have an address book sitting by a vase of flowers and your mother doesn't say, *Hey, kids let's call*

Uncle Ivan, let's send him a Christmas card, let's send him a gift for his new house in Specific Town, USA.

No, it's more like your mom stares into space and says, *Ivan went off to Idaho with his new girlfriend, who, by the way, is pregnant, so I guess that's that.* And you want to ask where, how pregnant, what does she mean, "that's that," and why. But she looks too sad and you don't want to bother her.

And when she says, *Fucking Roxanne and her twelve-step shit, I don't need anyone telling me what to do and I'm blocking her number so she gets the message,* you don't ask for a reminder about what Roxanne's last name is in case you ever leave home and have no one else to call.

Imagine that's how it is.

I picked up the phone and called information again and got a different person, a woman, and this time I asked to be connected to my school.

"A school? At this time of night?"

"Yes." I got through to the phone system and followed all the prompts to get to Mr. Bergstrom's voice mail, and then it disconnected me. It disconnected me and I didn't have the number because I'd been connected directly. I was about to call information again when I heard the key card in the door and Dixie walked in.

I put down the phone. She dropped the backpack on the floor and looked at me with a blank expression. Then she turned her back and went into the bathroom.

When she came out, I hadn't moved. She stood in front of me, waiting for me to say something. I could tell she expected me to be mad. To yell at her or be freaking out. But all I wanted to do was look at her. Her hair was kind of frizzed out the way it got sometimes in rain or fog, and her eyeliner had smudged under one of her eyes. I saw her as a kid, as a kid playing dress up in her Doc Martens and makeup and her hands shoved into her jacket pockets, defiant.

"Why are you looking at me like that?" she finally asked.

"Like what?"

"Like . . ." She pulled her hands out of her pockets and let her arms fall to her sides. "I was practically having a heart attack the whole time I was with Ryan. I kept waiting for him to try to get me to open it to prove there wasn't money in there."

"Did he?" I asked.

She shook her head. "I threw it in the trunk of his car like it really was full of your laundry." She pulled her jacket off. "We drove around. He wanted to show me the school where they all go. He kept telling me about the 'haunted dugout' or whatever at the baseball field, so we went there. We sat in it forever in the freezing cold and nothing happened. It was dumb."

She walked to her bed, picked up the TV remote, and dropped it again without turning the TV on.

"Nothing happened," she said. "I'm not what you think." She sat on the bed and unlaced her boots, took them off, let them drop onto the floor.

"What do you think I think?" I spun my chair around and used my heels to drag it over the carpet, closer to her.

She narrowed her eyes as I came toward her. "What are you doing?"

"What do you think I think?" I asked again.

"I think . . ." She pulled a pillow into her lap. "I think you think I'm mean. I think you think I'm a slut. I think you don't want me around. I think—" Her voice broke. She squeezed the pillow. "I think you think I'm a bad sister."

My instinct was to say no, you're not, and I started to, but Dixie continued. "I am. I stayed out as long as I could with Ryan while he bored me to death with his stupid stories because I wanted you think I wasn't coming back. I wanted you to know what it would feel like if I left." She brushed tears away with the back of her hand. "The way *you* want to leave. Leave me."

"It's not you that I want to leave."

"Then why, Gem? Why can't you *stay*?" She was tearful and urgent. "Because of Mom? She'll get better, you know she will. She always does. I mean, she always gets better enough, we always get by. We always do."

"I know." The only thing I could think to say was exactly what I felt, which sounded simple and selfish. "I can't go back. I want . . . I don't know. But I know I can't get it there, and I don't want to wait anymore. I'm ready now. I knew when I saw the money."

"Well, you don't have the money now. So you have to come back."

I scooted my chair even closer. Our knees touched.

"Why'd you give it to me?" Dixie asked, wiping her face again.

"Because you need it to go home."

"But what are you going to do? You need it more than I do."

I could see how she thought that, and I'd believed it myself even yesterday, but it wasn't true. She'd take it back to Mom and Dad, go home the hero, having gotten it back from crazy Gem.

"And," I said, "I wanted you to know I'm not like them. That it doesn't mean as much to me as you do."

She backed away from me and sat cross-legged in the middle of her bed, and pulled the pillow tighter, up to her mouth. I could only see her eyes. "I know. I know you're not like them."

"If you don't want to go back, if you think you shouldn't, I can . . ." I was going to say I could help her, but I didn't know if I could. I still didn't even know exactly how I was going to help myself. "I can find someone to help you."

She shook her head and set aside the pillow. "I told you. We always get by, Mom always gets better enough."

Enough seemed to be all she wanted. Maybe I needed too much, or maybe I wasn't strong.

No—that wasn't it. I think I'm strong. Or, more like I think whatever I am is okay. Maybe what I have is strength, or maybe what I have is weakness that I accept. Being strong is one way to be, but it's not the only way.

"You can't be mixed up in the pill thing at school anymore," I said. "For Mom or anyone else."

"I know."

"You can get a real job next year. And you have to focus on graduating and—"

"I *know*."

"I have to tell you something else," I said. "That you don't know."

She pulled the pillow into her lap again. "Okay?"

"There's some money missing. And Dad is going to be mad about it. More than the amount we spent on stuff." I wheeled my chair back a little bit. "I took seven thousand dollars of it. Then I accidentally threw it away with my old coat."

"Oh my god." She put her hand over her mouth. "Oh shit, Gem."

"Just tell him it's all my fault. Or I'll tell him. He can come after me. Let him try." I wasn't scared. I felt like nothing could happen to me ever again that would scare me.

She dropped her hand. "You took it? You weren't going to tell me?"

"It was, like, a backup plan."

"That you weren't going to tell me," she repeated.

"I know. I'm sorry."

A slow smile spread across her face. "That's kinda badass of you. I didn't think you could be that devious. Like me." Her smile fell; she looked down. "I thought you were the good one. I'm the bad one, you're the good one."

I took in her face, remembered how sweetly she trusted me when I used to tell her we were going to Narnia, going to Mars. How she always wanted to make sure our picnic rations were fair. How, whenever she drew us, we were holding hands.

"I don't think it works like that, Dixie."

"Yeah," she said. "Maybe not."

26

WE TRIED to get some sleep. We meant to stay right until checkout. But once we knew it was over, the idea of hanging out, ordering a pizza, watching more TV, didn't seem so fun. Dixie kept asking me what I was going to do. I told her I didn't know, specifically. I stayed vague. Our paths were going to diverge and whatever my plans were, her knowing them might not be the best thing for her or for me.

In the morning, while Dixie showered, I dug the burner phone out of the backpack and turned it on. It lit up with a message from Lia.

glad you're ok xoxo

She must have called or texted Lia the night before while we were separated. I fooled around with the phone until I could figure out how to see recent calls and messages, to see if Dixie had contacted anyone else. Dad, or Mom, or anyone. But she'd only texted Lia.

I looked at the contact list we'd programmed in since we got the phone:

mom

dad

lia

kip

I scrolled to Dad's number. My thumb hovered there. He'd been so out of my reach for so long—barely writing or calling all the years after he left, and not talking to me during the years he was there. I mean, he talked to me, but he didn't talk to me. He didn't ask me about me or give me helpful advice or read to me or sing to me or walk me to school or tell me I was good, tell me I was smart, tell me I was somebody worth something. I guess he could tell a different story about how it was, he could tell a version where he did those things, was a fine dad, not perfect, but not a total failure. He might even think he had a little evidence to prove it, too. The recital when he said I could sing. Getting us a cat before he left.

But no matter what he did or didn't do, he withheld himself. He withheld himself from me, my whole life. I wasn't the needy one now. He was. He needed to believe Mom would always take him back, he needed to believe he was going to be a big deal, he needed to feel important. It wasn't enough for him to just be there. Maybe that was the difference between me and Dixie, why I couldn't go back. She was willing to make the trade-offs, say what he or Mom needed to hear. At least for now.

Now, I had something he wanted. I could make him listen. And there was his number, him on the other side of a tiny movement of my finger. A simple thing for most people, maybe.

I pushed the call button. I lifted the phone to my ear and listened to it ring from a spot on my bed where I could see out the window. It was only a few rings before Dad answered.

"Yeah?"

"It's Gem."

He was silent.

"Gem, your daughter."

"Yeah, I know Gem, my daughter," he said. "Is Dixie with you?"

"Where'd you get the money?" I asked him.

"Do *you* have the money? Where are you? I need that back, Gem."

"Where did it come from?"

"It's . . . it came . . . I got it for my business. I told you I was starting my business."

"Did you steal it? Did you borrow it?"

He laughed. A kind of uncomfortable laugh that was more like holding himself back from yelling. "Sort of I borrowed it, I guess. That's why I need it back, I need to make a return on this guy's investment, you see? Where are you, sweetie?"

Sweetie.

"Don't be mad at Dixie."

He paused. "Okay."

"Everything was my idea."

"Just tell me where you are."

"We needed you." My voice shook. I swallowed and tried again. "We needed you. We really needed you to be better than you are."

He didn't say anything. I couldn't even hear breathing.

"Are you there?" I asked.

"Yeah. Yep."

"You can still try harder," I said. "It won't change anything for me. But maybe for Dixie. Maybe she'll give you a chance to be better."

I pressed the end button before he could say anything else, anything like *sweetie* or *honey* or *Gem, baby*. I turned the phone off and packed it away.

When we checked out, Dixie gave me the cash from the deposit—a hundred dollars. With what I'd had on me it added up to about two hundred eighty.

"How mad do you think Dad will be?" Dixie asked once we were outside and headed for the ferry. A thick blanket of fog made it so we could barely see down the block.

"Just keep remembering it's his fault, keep asking him where it came from, and if he gets mad about the seven thousand dollars, just ask him if he wants to report it to the police. He won't." I took her arm. "Don't let him push you around. You have to make yourself see through his bullshit."

She nodded. "Okay."

"And if anything gets worse or doesn't get a little better, tell someone, like Mr. Bergstrom. Or me."

She nodded again and hooked her thumbs through the backpack straps. I'd given her the phone, too. I didn't want any calls from Mom or Dad. I'd get a new one once we were back in the city.

We got our ferry tickets and waited, while the fog dissipated little by little. I loved being by the water, the way all the boats lined up in the docks, the different colors and the names of them—*Aurora's Borealis*, *Fishin Expe'dishin*, *Lucille*. I loved how the gulls soared in and out, and bobbed on the water not caring it was freezing cold. I loved the way the fog clung to just the very tops of the trees across the Sound, woven through the branches like cotton.

"I'm going to live on an island," I told Dixie. "Someday. In the future."

"Sounds boring," she teased.

"I'll have a little house. A little yard. A little dog."

"I'll visit," she said, "but you know I have to live in the city."

"Okay. You can visit."

It was too cold to stand on the deck. We got coffees and sat by a window, and scalded our tongues. She reached in her pocket and pulled something out. It was the picture, of me pushing her in the stroller.

"I found this with your stuff last night, when I was looking for the phone. I took it, in case I didn't see you again. But you probably want it."

I did want it. Even if there was someone else just outside the frame, even if the pose was a setup. It was still something true about us. She held it by its edge, looking at it closer. "You have to call me, too, if *you* need help. You can't, like, live on the street."

"I know. I won't."

She handed the picture back to me. I put it in my coat

pocket. My arm throbbed and sweated under the plastic wrap. I rolled up my sleeve and prodded it.

"In a couple days your tattoo will itch like a mother-fucker," Dixie said. "*Don't scratch it*. Keep it clean and moisturized. If it flakes a little, don't freak out; it's not coming off, it's just the top layer of skin."

"It looks good," I said.

"Yeah," she said. "It looks really good."

27.

DIXIE TOOK a cab home. There wasn't time for more of a good-bye than we'd had on the ferry, not with the driver watching and the meter going.

I got in a different cab and went straight to school, to Mr. Bergstrom's office. The door was closed. I knocked, and he opened it. I could see he had another student in there. I was so happy to see his face.

"Hi," I said, struggling against tears. "It wasn't fine."

When the other student had gone, I told him, "I found some money. I found this money and it seemed like . . .

it seemed like something that could help me with what I wanted."

"You found money? Where?"

"I—"

"Wait." He held up his hand and lowered his voice. "Legally, you're supposed to report found money. I mean, they don't really care if it's not that much, but it's basically theft. It wasn't that much, was it?"

What if you find it in your own house? Under your own bed?

"No," I said. "Not that much."

After that I worried what else I shouldn't say. I didn't want legal trouble. Maybe for my dad I wouldn't care. But for Dixie, for Mom, I didn't know the right thing to do. So I didn't tell him about the drugs, either. Everything else, though, I told. A lot of which he already knew. Feeling like home wasn't home, feeling like no one cared about me, feeling like I was the only responsible one in the family and worrying all the time that I should be doing something to make sure it didn't fall apart.

He wrote in his notebook while I talked. Then he asked, "Where'd you go? You missed some days of school. I was worried."

"I ran away," I said. "That's all. And I'm not going back." I'd been wrong when I thought I'd never feel scared again, because, in the middle of talking to Mr. Bergstrom,

I felt more scared than I'd been through the whole thing. Like a cage was going to drop down around his office and I'd be dragged home. "If anyone tries to make me go back, I'll leave again." I stood up and went closer to the door.

He put his pen down. His face had the goodness that I'd missed. "If neither of your parents reports you as missing, and you keep going to school, no one is going to come after you."

"They're not?"

"No."

"How come you never told me that before?"

He opened his mouth, then closed it and tilted his head. Then he said, "I realize this sounds incredibly inadequate, but you never asked. And you can understand I can't go around suggesting to students that they should leave home. Unless I know they're really in danger."

"Oh." I stared at my hands, ashamed to have thought my problems were so bad.

"Come sit back down."

I shook my head.

"I wish you'd trust me."

Not if he was going to keep using words like "legally." I felt for the handle and leaned against the door, my hand behind my back. "I know. It's not like I get hit. I don't get . . . touched. I don't get threatened."

"That's . . . good. That's good, Gem. I'm glad for that."

"Me and Dixie have our own room. My mom works sometimes. Enough to pay the rent. We don't always have food but I manage to eat."

He looked confused.

"What I'm asking is . . . You said you weren't supposed to tell me some things unless I was really in danger. What does it take to be really in danger?"

Mr. Bergstrom didn't say anything for a long time. He sort of rubbed his mouth with his hand and took some deep breaths.

"Gem? Please come sit down."

I didn't move. He brought me his box of tissues. "Here." I looked up. Was I crying? I touched my face. It was wet. I moved my hand off the door handle so that I could take a tissue.

"I don't flunk classes," I continued, my tears getting bigger, making it harder to talk. "I know I have problems in school and I know I'm antisocial, but I pull through every class."

"You do."

"I'm clean, I . . . I wash my clothes. I go to bed at bedtime and I wake up and come to school. And . . ." I pressed a tissue to my eyes and rocked forward. "I take care of my sister. For a long time I took care of her. I try."

"You do," he said, so kindly. "You try very hard."

"But . . . what does it take to be in danger?" I asked

again, through even more tears. "What does that even mean? Are things not bad enough? Should things be worse for me before . . . before I can make them better?"

I felt his hand on my arm, leading me back toward the chair. "No. No, they shouldn't." I sat down and he stood beside me, keeping his hand gently on my arm. "I'm sorry, Gem. I think I failed you."

I cried more when he said that, big crying that came with relief, like all I'd wanted or needed this whole time was for someone to say they were sorry and mean it. To notice what had gone unnoticed my whole life, what had fallen through the cracks.

When I'd gotten my breath back, he said, "I have some ideas. Why don't you give me some time alone here. Go to your classes and collect your homework assignments, get whatever you might need out of your locker. In case you need to take a few days off while we get you figured out."

"How am I . . ."

"I'm going to help you. You being older makes it easier than it would be if, well, if you were Dixie. Does she—"

"She doesn't want to leave."

"Right." He tapped his pen on the desk. "I think we can find some options. You know how I love to pull strings."

I nodded, and blew my nose a few times.

"I *will* have to actually confirm some stuff with your

mom. Just to avoid too much involvement from the system. Because the system sucks."

"But I don't want her to get in trouble. I don't want—"

"Let me talk to her." He smiled. "I'm a professional, okay? I'm good at these conversations and you don't even have to think about it. Not right now."

"Okay."

"Come back here when you're all set with your assignments and everything. And close the door behind you?"

So I went to my teachers, the ones I could find, and got the assignments I'd missed. Some of them looked at me funny and remarked that I'd really only missed a couple of days, like I was making a big deal out of nothing. I made them tell me anyway, and I also asked for ones that were coming up in case I missed some more days. Mrs. Cantrell was out; I got what I could from the sub. I asked if the reading journals had been handed back, but he didn't know what I was talking about.

My locker didn't have much in it. Two textbooks, a sweatshirt. I carried the things in my arms as the bell for passing period rang. Helena from my English class walked by, then stopped and turned around. "Hey. Gem."

"Hi."

"Where were you?"

"Sick," I said.

"Sick and . . . shopping?" she asked, pointing at my

new outfit. "I love that coat."

"Oh, thanks."

She tucked a strand of hair behind her ear. "Well, we have a *Grapes* test tomorrow, so."

"Grapes?" I asked.

"*Of Wrath.*"

"Oh. Thanks."

"Later, Gem," she said, and walked off down the hall as if it was just a normal day.

28.

MRS. MURPHY was a lady that Mr. Bergstrom knew from his church who used to take in older kids from the foster system but didn't anymore, not officially, not since she got divorced. Mr. Bergstrom got permission from Mrs. Harjo, the assistant principal, to drive me to her house. And also from my mom.

"How did she sound?" I asked him. "What did she say?"

We were pulling out of the teacher lot in his car, which was kind of old. You couldn't even see the backseat because of all the papers and boxes piled onto it.

"Well, she was upset."

I ran my finger through the dust on the dashboard. "She gets angry. If she feels like people are judging her."

"No, no, Gem, not angry. Upset. Like crying." He drove carefully, below the speed limit, it seemed like. "She's glad you're all right. She understood. I proposed it like . . . what we call 'respite.' That we have this person, vetted by the system, inviting you to stay so that your mom can have a break. I proposed it as a break for her."

I looked at him. "From me?"

"I know it's not entirely accurate, but it was the best way to get you the space you want."

"And I don't have to go back?"

He paused. "I can't promise that. We have to approach this as temporary—a break—unless you want to go through a whole different process with courts and all of that."

I didn't want that. Not if I could help it.

Mr. Bergstrom took his phone from the cup holder and held it out. "Why don't you call her? I think she'd like to hear your voice."

"I don't . . . I don't think I know her number."

He reached into the chest pocket of his shirt and pulled out a sticky note with a number on it and "Adri True" in neat printing.

"What should I say?" I asked.

"I don't know. What do you want to say?"

I held his phone, and the number. I looked out the window and saw how we were driving in green now, trees everywhere, like on the island.

"Can I just say that I'm all right and I'll talk to her more later?"

"Sure," he said. "That's fine."

I put in her number. "It's going to voice mail," I told Mr. Bergstrom. Her message didn't have her voice on it, only the opening of Stone Temple Pilots' "Interstate Love Song." I hung up.

"Do you want to try again?" he asked. "Leave her a message? I think you'll feel better if you do."

I tried again. She picked up. "Who's this?"

"It's me." There was a pause and I almost said *Me, Gem, your daughter*, like I'd done with Dad. But I should have known she'd know my voice a lot better than he did.

"Gem," she said.

I started crying again, when she said my name, not big like I had in Mr. Bergstrom's office but the second time in a day after going so long without, and weighed down by what I couldn't express. "I'm calling because . . ." My voice faltered; I couldn't finish the sentence. "Is Dixie okay?"

"Yeah, she is," Mom said. She sounded tired, she sounded small. "She's right here with me. I mean, she's asleep at the moment but we're together here at home."

I pictured Dixie in our room, just her, and my empty bed.

"I'm going to stay with this . . . with this lady for a while."

"I think that's good. Just until I kinda get my shit together, you know," she said, and then it sounded like she was crying, too.

I didn't know what to say, where to begin. "Me and Dixie were talking about that time we went camping. With Roxanne?"

Mom sniffled. "Yeah?"

"Remember that?"

"Sure I do."

Mr. Bergstrom reached into the backseat and handed me a box of tissues. I guess I was crying more.

"I'm going to try to work days," Mom continued. "So I can be here for Dixie at night. I should have . . . I don't . . ." She stopped, and when she started again, her voice was stronger, bigger. "I don't want you to worry about us. And if it's no good with that lady, if you don't like it, you come home." Another pause. "Okay?"

"Okay, Mom." I waited a second, then I said, "Bye," before there was too much space full of what she wasn't saying.

I put the phone back in the cup holder.

"That was good, Gem," Mr. Bergstrom said. He looked over at me and nodded. "That was really good."

Mrs. Murphy lived in a small two-bedroom house in Bellevue. She had two blue parakeets, Edgar and Edith, that she kept in the living room. They chirped whenever she talked and were quiet whenever I talked, tilting their heads to listen. "They like new voices," Mrs. Murphy said. She had gray hair in a bun, pleated jeans, and an over-sized beige T-shirt with a picture of a wolf on the front. Hiking sandals over socks. She was tall and heavy and capable looking.

She didn't talk for very long after Mr. Bergstrom left, and I hardly talked at all.

The tour of the house took only a few minutes. The furniture wasn't anything special. Everything was ruffled—the pillows, the curtains, the bedspreads.

"You'll sleep in here," Mrs. Murphy said, showing me the second room off the hallway. "I know it's small. Go ahead and throw those extra pillows on the floor if you don't want them."

"Is there a bus I can take to school tomorrow?" I asked. I'd decided I didn't want to miss any more days. There was the quiz in English, and Helena said she loved my new coat.

She tugged down on the hem of her T-shirt. "I told Mike—Mr. Bergstrom—I'd drive you to school in the mornings on my way to work, if you don't mind getting up with the birds. You'll have to take a bus home, though. Or, if you want, you could come to the library where I work to do your homework and I can bring you home." When I first heard "home," I thought of the apartment; then I realized she meant here, her house.

Tears rushed up. I turned from her and moved pillows around, sniffing, wiping my face with my sleeve.

"I'll leave you alone unless you need anything."

I nodded, and kept my back to the door until I heard it close.

I didn't sleep. My tattoo itched all night.

The only breakfast options she had were oatmeal and eggs.

"I like to keep my choices simple," she said. She wore the same high-waisted jeans and sandals with socks she'd had on the night before. This time her T-shirt was blue and had a bald eagle on it.

We decided on oatmeal. The parakeets had been moved into the kitchen with us. "They like to eat when I eat," she said.

I watched Edith and Edgar hop from the perch to their seeds, back to the perch, back to the seeds. "How can you tell them apart?" I asked.

"I can't always. Edgar is a liiiiitle bit bigger, aren't you, Edgar?"

Both birds chirped.

Dixie wasn't at school again until the next week. I saw her in the cafeteria, walking in with Lia and wearing her new leggings, a long-sleeved *Bleach* T-shirt, and her blue Docs. It seemed like forever since that day on the ferry. I crossed the cafeteria to her. Aside from maybe Lia— who was apparently good at keeping Dixie's secrets—I don't think anyone at school had any idea what was going on. No one looked at me or her any differently than they always had. I already felt more calm, though, less like something bad was about to happen.

"Hey," I said to Dixie and Lia.

"Hi," Lia said, a little nicer than usual.

Dixie said to Lia, "Save me a place in line." Lia left, and Dixie slipped her backpack off and knelt to the floor. She pulled out a plastic grocery bag, stuffed full. "I thought you might want some clothes." She held the bag out to me.

"Thanks," I said, and opened it to see what she'd brought. I didn't recognize anything. It was all new, with tags on. Some jeans, some T-shirts and hoodies.

"Me and Mom went shopping and I thought . . ." She shrugged.

"You went shopping? After everything we already spent?"

"Mom decided to let him pay back some of the child support. Well, more like she made him and said if he didn't, she'd tell someone about the money."

I didn't think they should be spending back child support on more brand-new clothes, but I took the bag and didn't say anything about it. Their problems weren't mine anymore. "Thanks. I've been washing this outfit like every night, so this is good."

"You'll like what I picked out. Gotta keep your new style up." She glanced across the cafeteria, then back at me. "What's it like at that lady's house?"

"I like it. She has pet birds."

She put her backpack on again and pulled a felt-tip pen out of her pocket. "Give me your hand."

I held out my palm. It was the arm with the tattoo, which showed because my sleeves were pushed up. The pen ink was cool and wet.

"This is the number of that phone we got. Call me when you get a new one so I have yours."

I nodded.

"Do you want anything else? From home?"

"No. You can get rid of everything, and have your own room, finally."

"What if you—" One of Dixie's guy friends had come running up behind her and grabbed her shoulders to surprise her. "Shit!" she shrieked. "Don't *do* that, asshole," she said, and pushed him away, laughing.

"I'll see you later," I said, before she could finish asking: *What if you come back?*

"Yeah," she said. "See you later."

29.

I KEPT adding little bits to my family history for Mr. Bergstrom. He didn't ask for it, but I found myself coming in with new pages almost every week. I was remembering more about my mom, more about my dad—sometimes good things that made me doubt myself again and wonder why I couldn't just have waited to leave until after graduation. Mr. Bergstrom reminded me that nothing and no one is all good or all bad, and that's what makes it so complicated. He also said I had a tendency to downplay my problems or compare them to other people's and that I shouldn't do that. He said people like me, with my kind of background, had to be careful to not abandon ourselves by thinking our problems are not important or not big deals. They can be big deals to us, even if they aren't to anyone else.

"Abandonment is what you learned," he said. "It will always be your first instinct."

Leaving, running. He says it will probably be something I'll want to do again at some point, but right now I find that hard to believe. I didn't want to leave Mrs. Murphy's that whole year, and no one made me.

Anyway, whether I remember a good thing or a bad thing, no matter how small it is, I add it to the history.

I remember how Dixie told me my dad said I had a good singing voice. I don't think she'd make it up.

I remember there was this one time from when Dixie was a baby and my parents were too tired to get up and make me breakfast, and I came into their room looking for them and they didn't get up but Mom said, "Just crawl in." She scooted over to make room for me. I climbed over her and lay down in the warm space between their bodies. We stayed there a long time.

That was all I had, but I was sure I'd think of more, remember more. At least I hoped I would.

I even did a part for my history all about Mr. Bergstrom, but I knew I wouldn't be able to get through it reading aloud without getting all emotional. So I just sort of stuck it in his hand right at the end of one of our appointments.

He worked hard with all my teachers to make sure I graduated. When I did, I wanted so bad to get him a present but I didn't have any money. After the ceremony, he gave me a little box and when I opened it later it had some gift cards for clothes, groceries, phone minutes. He asked if he could hug me and I said yes, and I couldn't help but cry a little bit. I think he did, too.

I ended up staying with Mrs. Murphy until I turned eighteen, through to graduation and some months after while I saved money. She helped me find out about programs and resources and things, and got me appointments with social workers and nuns. She introduced me to a girl—a young woman, I guess—Alicia, who had also lived with Mrs. Murphy, years ago. Now Alicia has her own apartment that she shares with two roommates, not that far from my old neighborhood. I'm closer to her than I am to anyone.

Nothing against Mrs. Murphy. We got along good. Life at her house was very quiet. She liked routines and peace and predictability—they worked for her like medication, she said. *My routines and my birds,* she'd say. They sort of worked the same for me. I told her about how I had tried, with little things—the way I arranged my room at home, my cigarettes—to create my own sense of peace, but the way life with my family was, those things hardly made even a small, peaceful dent.

"Oh, I can imagine," Mrs. Murphy said. "You were swimming upstream, that's for sure."

You're going to have enough shit to shovel your way out of down the line was how Uncle Ivan had put it that night in the hallway.

Though we didn't *talk* talk, the way I do with Alicia or even the way I used to with Mr. Bergstrom, I did tell Mrs. Murphy some things. And I learned from watching her and how she made a calm life. But Alicia understands my life without needing any explanation. And she helped me find a tiny studio apartment the way she did, through the same church where Mr. Bergstrom and Mrs. Murphy go. Catholics are really organized.

Right now I'm learning how to do a budget. I'm only supposed to spend a certain percent of my money on groceries, and I have food stamps to help, too, but I like to keep my refrigerator and cupboards as full as I can. I skimp on the heat and electricity, keeping the thermostat at 52 and not turning on any lights until the sun goes all the way down. I can always put on another sweatshirt if I'm cold.

I wanted to live on one of the islands. I asked Alicia if

she thought they could find me a place there but she said it's way too expensive for what I make now, and especially with my job being in the city, it's not a realistic option. That's fine. Maybe someday.

I'm taking a few classes at the community college. My heart's not in it that much, because I still have no idea what I want to do with my future other than picturing myself on an island, near water. Mostly I want to work and keep saving, because one thing I want to do is take a bus to Idaho to see Uncle Ivan and meet my baby cousin.

My job is thirty-two hours a week at a bakery that mostly does doughnuts. I go before dawn and tie on my apron and drink two cups of coffee to shake off sleep. I bake and frost, bake and frost, bake and frost, then work the register a little, too.

Dixie comes in sometimes and I give her my employee discount, with permission from my boss. I know what Dixie likes: the sunflower banana muffin. Or if we're out of that, a double-chocolate doughnut. She dyed her hair lighter blond recently and cut it short, and last time she came in she had a new tattoo on her wrist, a tiny mermaid, like the one Mom has near her collarbone. I wonder what Mom thinks of it, and of her hair, but I haven't asked Dixie, and when I talk to Mom we stick to the basics of how I'm doing and haven't figured out how to say much more.

Talking to Dad was almost easy—telling him, that time on the phone, that he should have been better, and then I felt free of him, like I could see him or not see him again and I'd be all right. With Mom it's different. Because sometimes she was good at being a mom. Those years when Roxanne was her best friend and they were going to meetings together . . . it really wasn't that bad. Like the camping trip. Or dancing around the living room together. That's what makes it harder with her. I don't expect anything from my dad but I think I still want something from my mom. Alicia says dealing with people that were sometimes good to you in the midst of being bad is like digging through piles of dog shit with your bare hands to find a couple of tiny nuggets of gold and no one wants to do that.

I kept smoking after the Haciendas ran out, which surprised me because I didn't think I was hooked. Mrs. Murphy didn't let me smoke at her house, but I'd find a little time between school and the library, and when I moved out I could do what I wanted. I still kept it to one a day. There are two left in my current pack—one for today, one for tomorrow. Then I'm quitting because it's expensive and unhealthy. I'd taken the Haciendas because they were my dad's and I wanted something of his. I'd wanted to be closer to some part of myself that's connected to him.

Now I've decided the cigarettes don't bring me closer to anything but my own nasty breath and a future case of lung cancer.

My manager at the bakery, Raúl, took forever to say my name right, *Gem* and not *Jim*. When I first started, I didn't even realize he'd been talking to me when I heard *Jim*. After I got more comfortable at work I told him, "It's Gem. With an 'e.'" And he said, "I know. That's what I'm saying. Jim." A lot of people say it like that, and I used to never correct them. I feel different now, about my name. Honestly I'd thought about changing it after everything happened, like my parents changed theirs when they were around my age, like Kip had changed hers. Something easy to say, something anonymous. Like Mary. Mary Smith. Mrs. Murphy said, "Oh no, no. Don't do that. You've got a good name. It's unusual and it means something." I'd never felt like it fit, I told her. I was too plain for it and not what my parents imagined when they gave it to me. "You might change your mind about that someday," she said.

Raúl is maybe forty-five or something, and big, and there are always sweat stains in the pits of his green bakery polo. My first couple of days at work, I was scared of him because his voice is loud and he doesn't smile a lot. But the other people on my shift—Jeff, Annie—kept saying stuff like *Oh, that's just how he is*, and teasing him, and telling me not to worry. Slowly I realized that, along with Mr. Bergstrom, Raúl is really one of the nicest people I've ever met.

"Hey, Gem, you were supposed to clock out ten minutes ago," he says now.

"I know. I'm meeting a friend and there's not time to go home in between, so I thought I'd stay."

"Clock out and get a doughnut and let's go sit down."

I take a buttermilk bar and put it in a bag, and Raúl and I sit at a corner table, him half-supervising Jeff.

"You're not going to eat that?" he asks, pointing to my bag.

"Not right now."

"So, who's this friend you're meeting?" Raúl leans heavily on his elbows, rocking the table toward him. "I thought we were your only friends. Right, Jeff?"

Jeff, from behind the counter, shrugs. "I guess she can have other friends."

I like how they tease me. Once I figured out they weren't making fun of me, that teasing is how they relate, it helped me feel like I belong.

"I do," I say. "Not a lot, but some."

Kip is on her first visit home since starting at Evergreen. It's less than two hours from Seattle, but she usually stays around the dorms on weekends. Even though I'm closer to Alicia now, Kip is still one of my best friends. When you have a shared experience with someone who showed you some kindness when you needed it most, it sticks with you. We're going to take the ferry together and hang out at her house tonight and tomorrow. Maybe go for a hike.

I get on ferries every chance I get—anytime the tip jar is a little more generous than usual or I need to see more trees. I usually stand on the outside deck for the whole ride unless it's pouring down rain, at least for as long as I can stand it. Steady in my boots, steady on my feet.

Sometimes I worry about Dixie. I can't help it. Dad is still in and out of her life, and Dixie still seems to get wrapped up in whatever he and Mom are into—their problems, their issues. Alicia is always reminding me I don't have the power to be responsible for every single person in the world.

"Not every single person in the world," I tell her. "Just Dixie."

"Still not your job," Alicia says. "Anyway, maybe what you're showing her by getting out of there, having your life now, is the best way you can help. You should think about that, Gem."

"Maybe."

Alicia says we'll always find each other, me and Dixie.

I know I can find Dixie. I wonder sometimes if she'll find me. Like I told Kip, she's the only other person in this world who knows what it is and what it was to be us. I don't know if Dixie really understands this yet, but when she's ready, I'm here. I'm staying right here.

Tonight when I'm at Kip's, we'll talk about it. We always end up talking about Dixie and Jessa because we both know a lot about sisters. We'll talk, and stay up too late, and then I'll sleep the deeper sleep I always get on the island. And I'll dream about living there one day myself, about boats and bicycles and water, and a dog running next to me on the road, in the green, green afternoon light.